"MY NAME IS KOLROTH. WELCOME TO MY SANCTUARY."

"This is Neron's temple!" you gasp, holding Ranger Gavin's arm for support.

"Once, but no more." Kolroth smiles as you are forced inside by his followers. "I am pleased you have come. I need a sacrifice for the full of the moon. You two will do nicely."

"Never!" Gavin shouts defiantly, lunging at the evil cleric.

Kolroth's men instantly jump him. "Run, Sword Daughter!" Gavin commands you, as you stand free.

But the troll still lurks in the darkness—and you don't want to leave Gavin alone. You have a desperate idea as you look around the temple of Neron. Surely some of the hero's favor with the gods still remains. Should you try to summon Neron's aid or run and leave Gavin to struggle alone?

If you try to summon ancient powers, turn to Pathway 21 (page 84).

But if you obey Gavin and leave him, turn to Pathway 49 (page 179).

Whichever choice you make, you will be exploring a new branch along your own private road to the Magic Realms. And no matter how your journey ends, when this adventure is finished, the fun will still go on. Just go back to the beginning of SWORD DAUGHTER'S QUEST and, by making different choices, you'll discover a whole new series of exciting and challenge-packed DRAGONTALES adventures.

DRAGONTALES

Choose a Pathway to the Magic Realms

(0451)

#1☐ **SWORD DAUGHTER'S QUEST by Rhondi Vilott.** While crossing the wastes on the way to the warrior games that will mark the start of your career as a swordswoman, your party is attacked by an orc raiding band, and your father is slain. Should you seek the help of the half-elven Ranger who rescues you and join his mission? Or should you follow the orcs by yourself? (130820—$1.95)*

#2☐ **RUNESWORD! by Rhondi Vilott.** Fleeing a pack of wolves, you stumble on the entryway to the mysterious mountain realm of the dwarf king. His kingdom is reputed to be filled with magnificent treasure. But beware! Many trials await you. Should you turn back now and seek help, or risk everything in search of wealth and the chance to master the legendary Runesword itself? (130839—$1.95)*

The dangers are great, but the rewards are too. It's up to you to make the choices and explore the many roads to magical adventure!

*Price is $2.50 in Canada

Buy them at your local bookstore or use this convenient coupon for ordering.

NEW AMERICAN LIBRARY,
P.O. Box 999, Bergenfield, New Jersey 07621

Please send me the books I have checked above. I am enclosing $_____
(please add $1.00 to this order to cover postage and handling). Send check or money order—no cash or C.O.D.'s. Prices and numbers are subject to change without notice.

Name _____

Address_____

City_____ State_____ Zip Code_____

Allow 4-6 weeks for delivery.
This offer is subject to withdrawal without notice.

DRAGONTALES #1

SWORD DAUGHTER'S QUEST

by Rhondi Vilott

Illustrations by Michael Gilbert

A SIGNET BOOK
NEW AMERICAN LIBRARY

NAL BOOKS ARE AVAILABLE AT QUANTITY DISCOUNTS WHEN USED
TO PROMOTE PRODUCTS OR SERVICES. FOR INFORMATION PLEASE
WRITE TO PREMIUM MARKETING DIVISION, NEW AMERICAN LIBRARY,
1633 BROADWAY, NEW YORK, NEW YORK 10019.

Copyright © 1984 by Rhondi Vilott Salsitz

Illustrations Copyright © 1984 by New American Library

Cover art by Tom Hallman

DRAGONTALES is a trademark of New American Library.

All rights reserved

SIGNET TRADEMARK REG. U.S. PAT. OFF. AND FOREIGN COUNTRIES
REGISTERED TRADEMARK—MARCA REGISTRADA
HECHO EN CHICAGO, U.S.A.

SIGNET, SIGNET CLASSIC, MENTOR, PLUME, MERIDIAN and NAL BOOKS
are published by New American Library,
1633 Broadway, New York, New York 10019

First Printing, July, 1984

1 2 3 4 5 6 7 8 9

PRINTED IN THE UNITED STATES OF AMERICA

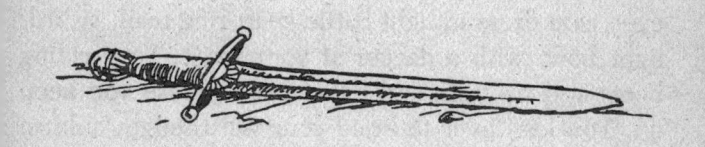

The hot sun beats down on you even as it begins to dip toward the mountains. You shift in your saddle as your father, General Hamroth, orders, "Halt, Sword Daughter!"

You look inquiringly at him. He motions you to dismount, saying, "We're going to camp early tonight."

The caravaners who have been guiding you across the colored sands and rocky terrain of the wastes are already making camp. They use their robes and banners as tents against the sun. Their leader, Ranth, salutes you and your father. "Great general," he says, "we are ready for the Warden."

"Good." Hamroth turns and answers your question before you can ask. He puts an arm affectionately about your shoulders. "My curious Tyrna. The Warden comes from the high elves who look after the valleys to the south. He must pass judgment on us

5

before we can go on." He adds, "Change into battle dress. I want a full exercise from you before sunset."

You groan, both at the delay and at the exercise, but you stop as you see your father's eyebrow rise. You remind yourself that the reason you've come across the wastes is to toughen you on your journey to the Warrior Games. Under Hamroth's watchful eyes, you dress in light battle gear: ring mail, sword, light bow, with a dagger at your waist. Your riding boots and trousers and full-sleeved blouse you keep on. You lean over to braid your waist-length auburn hair so that you may tuck it under the lightweight helmet.

"Father," you ask as you step into the light of the bonfire, "the sky grows dim. Will we have time to visit the temple of Neron?"

You're anxious to see the monument to the paladin Neron who battled the blue dragon Slag alone, without the aid of any but the gods. After a fierce fight, he threw the beast down from the Arad Mountains. The spot where the dragon died became a mighty spring, which spills into a lake and then runs across the desert as the river Ashkaraneth. Someday, you hope, you will do something as glorious as Neron!

Hamroth shakes his head no. "I don't think so, Tyrna. It's dangerous here and we can't linger. Slag left more than destruction behind—he left a path of great evil that attracts others. Neron deserves our tribute, but we should hurry on our way. Besides, you need to get to the Warrior Games on time, or you'll have to wait until next year to begin your training. And next year..."

"I know. You're worried it may be too late by then," you finish for him. You give him a light kiss. "Don't worry, Daddy. I can be a girl and a fighter too. No one is going to steal my heart." At least, you think, not until I've had the chance to do exciting things and perhaps win a great fortune! The only exciting thing your father has left from his career is a gift from the elves, a cloak of concealment. He carries it everywhere with him. You think it is a wonderful thing to own, but there are many other wonderful things in the world.

Your father sighs. "Don't be too sure of that. I thought I could be a father and a husband and a general, but your mother did most of the work for me. It wasn't until she was gone and I had to take care of you myself that I realized how hard it could be. Now, quit stalling! I will not have you out of shape and a disgrace at the games!"

You take a deep breath and, with a salute, you begin the exercises he has taught you to train your body and your mind for a fighter's life. Though it seems you draw your sword against shadows, each movement stretches and tones your muscles. You are small but wiry. Your father has taught you to be agile and daring as you leap and jump. Your imaginary opponents scatter.

Screams tear the night. The caravaners run in confusion as war yelps sound from what must be orcs! Your father jumps to his feet, grabbing his elven cloak of concealment. He throws the cloak about you before drawing his sword.

"Stay down, Tyrna!" he commands, running into the night, his sword readied to protect the fleeing caravaners.

Your heart beats wildly in fright! But you can't let your father fight alone, one against so many orcs. They crash through the night around you, gnashing their tusks and chasing the terrified caravaners. They can't see you as you race after your father, but your sword hangs in front of you as though enchanted. They yelp in fear. You feel a little guilty—it is not a fair battle—but the orcs are swarming everywhere. You must help your father!

Even as you reach his side, the orc leader howls in triumph. Hamroth's sword wavers. He has been wounded! You step in front to protect him from another blow as the orc swings a mighty club. Great pain and fire flashes through your head, and you sink into darkness.

You awaken, cold water stinging your face. You look into the most beautiful violet eyes you have ever seen. A man bends over you, but he is no one you know. His hair is like sunlight, and you blink in bewilderment at the sight of pointed ears. The expression in his eyes is stern.

"Father?" you ask, but your voice is still weak. You have forgotten what has happened. You struggle to sit up. "You are . . . elven!"

"Yes, luckily for you. How else could I have seen you still alive under that cloak of yours?"

Tears sting your eyes as you look around and remember the desert battle. Your father's body is surrounded by many slain orcs. You hold back your sorrow, thinking that he would have wanted to die this way, honorably defending others.

As your rescuer helps you stand, you see he is taller than you. Your chin reaches his broad shoulders. He cannot be a true elf! Your father's warning of evil in the wasteland makes you suspicious. You put your hand on your sword's hilt. "Who are you?"

"Gavin, Warden of these wastes. And you must be Tyrna, Hamroth's daughter. The caravaners sent messengers ahead days ago to let us know you would be crossing."

You eye him suspiciously. "Then you're the one we were waiting for when the orcs struck us."

Gavin looks down at you, unsmiling. "You forget I have elven blood in me. I, too, hate orcs. I came to protect you."

"You were too late!" Sadly, you bend to gather the goods scattered from your pack. You notice that few of the bodies are caravaners, though dead orcs lie everywhere. Ranth and his tribesmen have disappeared.

As you look, footprints and a faint trail show that the orcs have taken the caravaners prisoner. You shudder at the thought of the horrors the caravaners must be experiencing. Better to die than be enslaved by orcs! Your father's death was in vain unless you rescue them!

Quickly, you retrieve his sword. Gavin knocks it from your hand. "Take nothing! The orcs will be back. They remember every piece of loot they have left behind."

You stare. Already, you miss your father terribly. You have nothing left of him but the elven cloak and memories. You cannot let his death to defend the caravaners be useless. You must go after Ranth and his tribesmen. You don't think the cold-natured Warden will understand your grief and fury. How can an elf understand human emotions? "I must do something!"

"What can you do?"

You don't answer right away. You mistrust Gavin. Is he who he says? Murderous orcs don't seem to bother him, though elves and orcs have warred countless generations. You have the trail sign clearly before you. Perhaps it would be best for you to go on alone after the caravaners.

Yet even if you found the orcs, you would be outnumbered. You have a lot to learn about fighting—and, truthfully, you don't have much stomach for killing after last night. It was not as glorious as you had imagined. You think of Neron and his temple. Perhaps you could get aid there, from pilgrims or maybe even the spirit of the paladin himself.

Or, you think, you could stay with Gavin and hope he will help you. You hesitate, unsure of what to do.

Gavin touches your shoulder. "You must do nothing," he repeats sternly. "We must leave immediately in case the orcs return."

"I can't leave! I want to avenge my father!" you cry, pointing your sword to the heavens.

"You are one sword," he says, watching your face. You feel uncomfortable, for there is a strange expression on his. "What can you hope to do?" He waits for your answer. You must decide.

1. *Will you trust Gavin and accompany him, hoping he will want to rescue the caravaners also? Go to Pathway 14 (page 59).*
2. *Trail the orcs on your own? If so, turn to Pathway 1 (page 12).*
3. *Or go to Pathway 33 (page 126) to ask Gavin to take you to the temple of Neron so that you may find help in your quest of rescue and vengeance?*

PATHWAY
1

"I'll see them roast before I quit!" you answer, as the sun strikes your blade.

"I see. Well, the heart filled with the need for vengeance feels little else," Gavin answers, turning away. "I will not help you with your quest."

"Cold elf!" you accuse, afraid of being alone and angry at his rejection of your need to have your father's death avenged. Disregarding his earlier words, you pick up your pack and the few items left, arrows, oil for your weapon, a water skin, and a package of the dry, mealy journeycakes that the caravaners made. You break into a jog, following the faint trail on the sands.

You sense Gavin behind you. Despite your distrust, you wish that he had come along. You don't wish to be alone in the wilderness. Also, you found his face not . . . well, not unpleasant to look at.

Gavin comes up beside you. "This is foolishness, Tyrna. What if the orcs double back?"

"Then I'll spit them that much faster!"

"And when you run out of water?"

"Then I'll dig pits in the sand and hope they gather moisture, or that the orcs and I meet sooner!" You look over at his moving in stride with you. You notice that your head barely tops his shoulders, though you are not tall for a human. He is terribly tall for an elf. Pushing the effect of his looks from your mind, you add angrily, "I won't leave anybody to the mercy of the orcs. I've got to rescue the caravaners."

He says nothing in answer. He paces you. The hot sun doesn't seem to bother him as he runs lightly over the rocks and sand. You, on the other hand, begin to regret your brashness. Your head has begun throbbing where you were hit. It pounds with every step you take. Besides, you have more problems to worry you. Though you won't admit it, you fear the water skin you have picked up is empty! But you don't want to slow down. The last thing you want to do is tell Gavin you were wrong . . . he'd probably send you home.

Should you risk being sent home or admit you are having difficulty?

1. *If you think you should stop and tell Gavin that you are in pain and need water, go to Pathway 31 (page 121).*

2. *Knowing that you cannot afford to be sent back, will you decide to tough it out? If so, see Pathway 34 (page 129).*

PATHWAY 2

"If you think it's safer, then boat it is," you agree wearily.

Gavin's eyebrow rises. "No argument?"

"None." You watch as Gavin affectionately rubs Stormseeker's neck and bids him goodbye.

He begins to drag the small boat into the water. The name *Arrow* is painted on the bow. You grasp the side and help, though you must wade in up to your knees. As you enter the boat, Gavin pushes it into the current and jumps in, grasping his pole.

The sun dips below the Arad Mountains, giving the wastelands a dark gray-and-pink tinge that grows ever deeper as you near the lake. Gavin sings quietly, an elven tune that lulls your mind. The effort of poling the boat becomes great, though. He pauses from time to time and flexes his neck and shoulder muscles.

"Let me take a turn."

"No." Though you can't see him, you imagine he is smiling in the dark. "You've been busy enough today."

Before you can protest, he shushes you. "Quiet. Listen. Sound carries a long way on the water."

Soon, you hear what he has heard. Orcs! They're raucous, yelling and cursing. You can see their bonfires on the horizon. Are they roasting the caravaners? Not likely, but the thought makes you shudder.

Gavin leans close to whisper, "We are nearly at the lake. Overboard here, and we'll walk it to shore."

He poles it close so that you do as he says, and the two of you guide the little boat into the reeds and anchor it there.

"Good going," he says.

"Thanks—" you begin, interrupted as orcs jump through the brush! They are on Gavin before he has a chance to pull his weapon.

You throw your hands in the air as spears point at your chest. Your heart is beating so loudly you think they must be able to hear it.

"Kill him—he's elf. Scratch don't like elves."

"Naw." A large orc strolls up, cuffing the guards aside. He stops by Gavin. Gavin rolls away from a swift kick in the ribs. You start forward, thinking of helping, but the spear points stop you. The Ranger rubs his side ruefully as he gasps.

"Kill elf now! More fun!"

The largest of the group grins from ear to ear, a nasty smile. "Never! More fun to torture elves than it is to kill! Remember problem we have in new

15

tunnel? Torg thinks he has just found solution. Good!" He kicks Gavin again. "Get up!"

Bound and gagged, the two of you are marched to the lake's edge. Torchlight illuminates a huge wooden structure that is being built where the lake flows into the river, slowing it to a trickle. Gavin growls as he sees it. They are slowly but surely damming up the sacred river.

You are marched down inside the excavation at the base of the watergate. The orcs have been tunneling here. Passageways run in all directions. The caves are beautiful colors, pink and purple and bright yellow, and pure-white crystals reflect back at you. As you near a tunnel, the air becomes more and more blue. Even the walls appear blue.

Torg grins horribly as he slices your gags off. He motions the two of you forward.

You and Gavin look at each other and start down the tunnel, spear points encouraging you.

"What can it be?" you cry, thinking of all the monsters that inhabit the subterranean levels.

"I don't know," Gavin replies, "but it can't be worse than orcs behind spear point!"

He's wrong, as suddenly you stumble into a cavern and a hungry blue dragon rears up, his mouth opening to blast you with his lightning-bolt breath!

END ADVENTURE

PATHWAY 3

"**T**omorrow will have to be good enough," you answer tiredly. "I don't think I can walk or ride another step."

Gavin smiles. "All right then. We'll camp here and ride up in the morning." He pats Stormseeker on the neck. "Go find water and grass, my friend."

The stallion trots off with a whicker. You watch him go.

"Doesn't he ever get tired?"

"Yes." Gavin answers slowly. "Evil wears him down. And, when we get home, he will have to rest for many days." He takes his pack off and throws it down. "Can you do without a fire?"

"Of course. I'm a Sword Daughter, remember?"

"Good. Then you won't mind a dinner of journey-cakes and water," says Gavin as he pulls a packet out.

You share the cakes baked especially for long trips, but the magical taste of the Ashkaraneth makes them lighter and better-tasting than anything you have had in a long time. Gavin folds his cloak and makes a pillow out of it for you. As the night becomes deep and dark, he takes something else from his pack. He puts the long thin object to his lips and blows a light tune on it. It is a whistle, but unlike any you've seen before. It gives a high sweet song, like a reed flute.

The music lulls you. You watch him as he plays, thinking of all the emotions you feel inside you for the first time. Would your father understand? You hope that he would. As you close your eyes and settle into sleep, you wonder if you are falling in love.

Morning birds and Stormseeker's wet muzzle wake you. The horse nudges you again and tosses his head. Gavin is already up. He smiles. "The lake is clear. Go wash your hands and face and we'll be off."

With Stormseeker guarding you, you get ready for the day's ride. As Gavin boosts you aboard the stallion's back, he says, "We'll be at the top in late afternoon."

"Why so late?"

"Stormseeker's power won't be any good climbing that mountain path. He can only go as fast as any mortal horse." Gavin smiles. "Don't worry. We'll get there."

Holding tightly to his mane, with Gavin running lightly beside you, you begin the ride into the Arad Mountains. It's another hot day. Evidence of Slag's destruction is all around you—trees made of stone and the ground melted like black glass. Stormseeker trots cautiously through the mountains.

The day seems to pass swiftly as you go higher and higher. Just as you are beginning to fret that you won't make it, Stormseeker stops suddenly.

You straighten to see the shadows of the mountain. A massive landslide blocks the path ahead. There is no way to get around it.

Gavin strokes the horse's neck. "I'm sorry, Tyrna. We'll have to go back and climb."

You turn the horse and make the long ride back to the base of the mountain. It is late now and the shadows stretch across the foot of the climb as you ride up.

Turn to Pathway 45 (page 165).

PATHWAY
4

You simply put your hand into his. "I have no choice."

He looks at you with happiness and astonishment lighting his elven face. You think how handsome he is and turn your face away, afraid he will be able to read your mind. But he puts his fingers under your chin and forces you to look into his eyes.

"Thank you, Tyrna. I'll see you have your vengeance as Sword Daughter—but remember, the heart can't live on revenge. I'll give you much more . . . once all this is over."

You remember your father's fears that just such a thing might happen to you as you are swept with feeling. You realize that, in this at least, your father was wrong. Falling in love is the best and most glorious thing you could ever have wished!

Gavin pats Stormseeker. "Away, my friend. We'll

call when we need you." And the stallion whisks away in a thunder of hoofbeats.

On foot and very cautiously, Gavin leads you to the orcish dam. It is sunken deep into the earth. Though the opening is new, as you enter it, it is obvious that the tunnels here have nothing to do with the dam. They were created when the world was very young and not by nasty orcs. As your perception dims, Gavin leads you on.

The ground is cold. Its sense of age makes a chill go down your spine, and you shudder. You feel that something evil has abided here in the depths. Slag's nest must have been here somewhere.

Gavin senses your shudder. He stops, his warm body shielding you. "Don't worry. The treasure holds the malice from the old beast yet. Legends of dragon gold poisoning men's hearts and souls are true! But the sun can wash it clean, if men know how before they are corrupted."

He pulls you forward with him again. Your footfalls echo in the dark faintly.

Suddenly, Gavin stops and pulls you to the tunnel side with him. You press against the wall. The sounds and shuffles of other steps deep in the earth reach you.

"Orcs?" you whisper, but Gavin holds you close and tells you to be silent.

After a long moment, he edges forward again. As you follow, you can see slightly. The tunnel ends, forking into other passages. There is a cleft nearby that an orc could not squeeze into. Torches sputter in their holders on the wall. Other creatures besides orcs must be down here, the caravaners, perhaps, or maybe the creatures have a human leader. You have heard of renegade fighters banding with orcs.

Gavin slips your elven cloak out. "I need this," he says, "and you will not need it again, if my plan works."

You grasp its edge. It is really all you have left that reminds you strongly of your father. But you realize that the past is already far behind you. You let go reluctantly. Gavin's face bends near as you whisper, "Then take it."

You know he has some daring plan in mind. You wonder what it would be like to kiss him goodbye for luck. There is nothing to stop you. You hesitate, wondering if you should kiss him or not.

1. If you wish to kiss him, turn to Pathway 40 (page 150).
2. See Pathway 28 (page 111), if you decide not to.

PATHWAY 5

You push away from Stormseeker's back, just as the stallion swerves to avoid a chuckhole. You are unceremoniously dumped—far from where you had intended to jump!

"Tyrna!" Gavin yells in fear.

Chills race down your neck as you break into a run, hearing the stampede right at your back! You sprint your fastest, but you know you aren't close enough to make it!

You pivot. A bull leading the stampede rolls his crazed eyes. He sees you! He lowers his horns and charges directly at you. You freeze, your heart pounding. What can you do?

"Run, Tyrna! Run!" yells Gavin desperately.

The bull is nearly on top of you and lowers his head even more to impale you on his horns. You take a deep breath and reach out, grabbing his horns. As

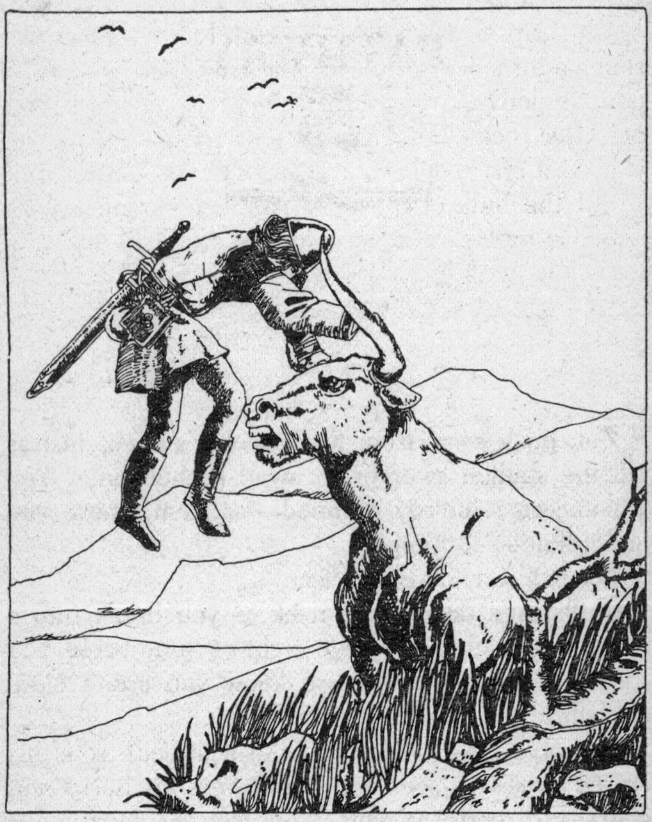

he tosses his head up in surprise, you jump and are airborne, somersaulting over his head and onto his back—just like the famed bull dancers of old!

You grip tightly to his powerful neck. It is like riding a tornado, but the animal can't shake you as he pounds along in front of the stampede. As he swerves past the rocks and embankment protecting Gavin, you vault off. Gavin breaks your fall with a grunt.

But the bulk of the herd is still booming toward you. He pulls you down onto the soft dirt, and protects you with his own body. The roar of cattle's hooves surrounds you, their voices bellowing and panting as they pass.

Suddenly, the soft ground under you opens up and you are dumped below, into darkness!

The earth has swallowed the two of you whole. Even as you gasp for breath and cough, Gavin grips you tightly. You are too stunned to say anything as he cradles you and calls your name softly. Your face is pressed to his broad chest, and you listen to the racing of his heart. A feather-light kiss brushes your temple as he calls your name softly again. He must care for you, you think in wonder. You stir and sneeze.

He releases you instantly. "What kind of stunt was that?" he says angrily. "You could have broken your neck!"

You are confused. Here he is, all angry again! You stand up quietly and shake the dust off. As you look around, you see you have fallen far, far underground. There is a small patch of sunlight above you. Even if you wanted to climb back up, it is uncertain if the cave-in will support you. It might come down even worse.

Gavin groans suddenly. You shudder. You're afraid of the dark and a little afraid of him, too.

Gavin stands and dusts himself off. He touches the walls. "This is a freshly dug tunnel. The walls have been partially excavated. No wonder it gave way under the stampede. It saved our lives."

You can't see as well as he can because of his elven senses. But you can smell a strange, musty odor, almost like that of thunder and lightning on a rainy summer day.

Your hand is captured by Gavin, and he gives a reassuring squeeze as you ask, "Where are we?"

"I'd say very close to where the orcs are building the dam. Let's get out of here. I don't want to try climbing out. Let's see what's up ahead. I'll guide you."

The crack above lends a dim light as you wend your way through the catacomb. Soon, the tunnel ends in a cave-in of light rocks and soil. The two of you dig through it. As you do, your sight becomes clearer. You are near a fork of two more passages. One leads to your right and is clearly lighter. The second, to the left, is lit with an eerie light-blue glow. You immediately prefer the light tunnel on the right.

"Let's go that way."

Gavin shakes his head. "It stinks of orcs! Though it's weird-looking, I'd say the blue tunnel might be better. I don't want to run into the raiding party just yet—not until I get my bearings down here. I don't want us trapped!"

"Orcs are why I came!" you declare.

Which tunnel will you take?

1. If you decide to avoid the orcs and take the blue tunnel, go to Pathway 41 (page 153).

2. Since orcs are why you came and you want to take the light tunnel, turn to Pathway 9 (page 42).

PATHWAY 6

Stormseeker paws the ground as though he senses you are unhappy.

"Please help me," you beg of the horse, but he does nothing. You realize that you must help yourself. "Oh, Gavin! You must let me go with you. Don't ignore me because I'm female! Why, some of your best elven fighters are women. You, of all people, should be the last to condemn me."

"I should? I, Gavin, the half-breed, half elf and half human?" he answers with a laugh. "I know less than half about anything!"

Stormseeker circles about the two of you as though surveying you from all angles. You continue trying to convince the Ranger.

"You know that orcs are trouble. One will fit as neatly between two swords as spitted on one. Give me a chance!"

He looks away from you, his dark violet eyes troubled. "I cannot," he says finally.

"But why?" you cry desperately.

You have forgotten Stormseeker. Suddenly, his broad head butts you in the back. You stumble and fall into Gavin's arms. He catches you and then, for a moment, holds you tightly. You are stunned by his embrace.

Just as suddenly, the Ranger releases you and turns away. "That is why!" he says. "You'll be in my way. From the first moment when I saw that you weren't dead and you opened your eyes—that somehow the orcs had overlooked you—I've been caught. The human half of me wars with the elf! I can't take you, Tyrna!"

You are stung. You had felt something of the same for him. It bewilders and frightens you. All you can do is remember the love your mother and father had and what your mother used to say, years ago: "The greatest heroes are those with heart."

You don't say any more, because you don't wish him to know you are also attracted. If he knew, you're afraid he would be even more determined to keep you from harm's way.

"Stormseeker!" You whirl toward the horse. "Tell Gavin that it isn't the stallion who leads the horse herd, but the wisest mare, while the stallion protects the rear. We'll be stronger together!"

The horse nods his head, his mane billowing. Gavin, both anger and joy showing in his face, says roughly, "I am overruled, then. We can't stand in the open any longer. Mount up!"

He opens his pack and drops a seed into the ground beside your father's body.

"What are you doing?"

Gavin smiles toward you, answering, "Leaving a tribute for you." He pours a tiny amount of water from his canteen. "This is water from the Ashkaraneth. It is special, yet always different."

As the water soaks the ground, a green shoot breaks through. It grows rapidly, twisting toward the sun, branching out until a tree shades the battleground. Green leaves break forth. Then huge golden blossoms cover the branches.

"It's beautiful!"

Gavin joins Stormseeker. "It will bear fruit later. As long as I or someone waters it from the Ashkaraneth every season, it will shelter and comfort travelers across this land."

Without another word, Stormseeker breaks into a lope and Gavin strides beside him as you travel toward the mighty Ashkaraneth and your goal, hidden in the Arad Mountains on the horizon.

The day is long. Gavin runs lightly, easily, beside you, and you talk of many things. He tells you of the beauty of the green valleys where he lives and where the Ashkaraneth has brought life back to the land.

You tell him of your father. He says, "I've heard of Hamroth. He was well spoken of, by elves and men."

You remember the elven cloak. Gavin stowed it in his pack before you left. "Was the cloak a gift from your valley?"

"No, but we elves have a way of knowing what happens."

You ride Stormseeker in silence. You're glad that Gavin knows of your father and wish that Hamroth could have met the Ranger. Then you blush and hope he has not seen it!

A thin blue line crosses the desert. Gavin points. "The river! We will be there in a few more strides."

"But we aren't that close!"

He slows, and Stormseeker stops to let him catch up. The Ranger laughs. "Tyrna! Surely you've noticed! We've come a long way since we started. Even elves can't run like that!"

You look back. Gavin is right. The tree has disappeared and nothing familiar is in sight. "What happened?"

"That's one of Stormseeker's gifts. He helps me find trouble, wherever it may be, and when I run or ride with him, I can travel leagues at a single stride. How else can you catch up with a storm?" He laughs, as though it is a special joke, and Stormseeker whinnies. He stops, watching you.

You turn away suddenly, afraid that you might blush or that your hair is coming free. Stormseeker begins to lope again, and Gavin joins him. You hold tightly onto the horse's long, silken mane and wonder why your heart is pounding so.

The river appears before you. You're disappointed; it is scarcely more than a wide stream. Gavin kneels before it.

"It is low! The river is drying up!" he says angrily. "This will mean a terrible drought." He stands. "I must hurry and get you to the temple. I can't wait much longer to find out what's happening."

"I'm sorry, Gavin."

He pats your booted foot. "It's not your fault, Tyrna."

Soon you are at the base of the massive, purple mountains that rise abruptly from the desert sands. There is little greenery here. Stormseeker lowers his head and crops a few shoots of growing grass. The land looks black and hard. You've seen rock like that—as though from a volcano. Gavin helps you down from Stormseeker's back.

"What happened here? It looks as though the mountains were burned."

"They were—by Slag. Blue dragons breathe a lightning bolt, instead of fire. He laid waste here many times to the men and elves and dwarves who came to kill him. After a while, no one else was brave enough to come—until Neron." Gavin points up the mountain. "Stormseeker can't make it up there. We can climb from here, taking a shortcut, or we can ride around into the mountains and take the pass. It's late, though, and we couldn't ride until tomorrow. Even Stormseeker gets tired."

The stallion shakes his head vigorously as though denying it, but Gavin laughs at him.

You know that Gavin is in a hurry, as are you. However, you are tired and the mountain looks sharp and unfriendly.

If you elect to climb, see Pathway 45 (page 165).
Go to Pathway 3 (page 17) if you decide to ride around.

PATHWAY 7

"All right," you say. "The falls it is."

Gavin does not bother to disguise his sigh of relief. He boosts you back up on Stormseeker, as the horse seems to dance in relief, too.

As you circle the lake, with its deep, sapphire-blue waters, you can see the falls more clearly. From out of nowhere, from bare rock, the waters arch. The air is filled with their sound, almost like singing.

Gavin halts Stormseeker at the base of the mountain. He helps you down—and is it your imagination, or do his hands linger at your waist for the barest of moments? Flustered, you kneel at the lake and wash your face as he bids his steed goodbye.

You are terribly tired, but the water feels alive in your hands. As you splash it over your desert-chapped face, the coolness heals and soothes. Despite your redhead tendency to sunburn, you feel great! But you stand as Stormseeker whickers a soft farewell and gallops off.

"Won't we need him? What are you doing?"

Gavin smiles. "He'll come when we call. He won't be far, but I don't want him out here in the open, where hunting orcs might spot him. They like horseflesh."

You shudder. Just one more reason why the poor caravaners need to be helped quickly! You stretch your head back and look over the cliff you must climb to reach the falls. It is broken, with plenty of foot- and handholds, but the rainbow spray of the waters has dampened it. Before you can protest, Gavin starts up. He holds his hand out to you.

"Come on . . . I'll help."

You grit your teeth and start climbing yourself. Before long, both of you are barely moving. You think of yourself as a spider, inching slowly and patiently along the wet rocks. Gavin is nearly as out of breath as you are, but he pauses long enough to throw you an encouraging smile.

"You're doing well," he says.

You wipe your forehead. As you do so, a rock slips free, and it bounces noisily a long way down. You and Gavin freeze, clinging to the cliff. But there is no one about to hear the noise. He takes a deep breath.

"Are you all right?"

"Yes," you answer, shaken. That could have been you falling!

He touches your hand. "Nearly there."

Another few feet and as you look up, Gavin is pulling himself up to the ledge beside the falls. You wait, your heart pounding. The rocks are tremendously slippery. Your fingers are cut trying to find a grip. As he pulls himself up, boulders tear at him. He cries out sharply.

He is caught! His pack has become entangled on the outcropping. He can neither scramble forward to safety on the ledge, nor can he drop back.

"Wait! I'll be there!" you call, as you quickly scrabble upward. But before you can reach him, he gives a tremendous heave.

The strap tears and the pack falls away. It lands in the Ashkaraneth with a splash, and foaming waters swirl it away. You twist to watch. It bobs up against the lake's bank and comes to rest there. Even as you look, the pack rips open as green shoots suddenly tear through it. Branches sprout everywhere!

Gavin groans. You look up in amazement. "What's happening?"

"Seeds. I brought them for planting, before I knew there was trouble. The waters of the Ashkaraneth do that. But I didn't intend this. Now the orcs will know that elves have been at the lake."

"Oh, Gavin," you cry in answer, as you look back at the miraculous greenery, now a stand of tall saplings, "they're beautiful! Maybe the orcs won't even notice."

"I hope not—at least, not until we're out of here."

He lies down on the ledge and looks over at you, extending his hand. "Come on, let's get going."

You take his warm, strong hand and he pulls you up. As you stand beside him, you take one last look at the trees brought from seed in minutes. Truly the Ashkaraneth must be a wonder of the world!

Gavin stands at the mouth of the tunnel. The falls thunder at your back, wetting you with a light foam. "Still want a torch?"

You hesitate, but only a second. "No, but you'll have to lead the way."

A smile lights his face as he holds out his hand to you again. You grasp it and are grateful that he cannot see you blush as the two of you enter the cave's twilight.

You stumble. He catches you up quickly. Your heart pounds as he sets you back on your feet. But his arms remain encircled about you. You sense his face bending low over you—is he going to kiss you? But he pauses and says quietly, "Later."

Your knees shaking a little, you follow him farther down the tunnel. Later what? You hope you know!

After what seems like a lifetime, the tunnel has begun to dip downward. You find it hard to keep up with the tireless Ranger. You sense that the walls are high. The tunnel must be huge.

"Why is it so big?" you whisper.

Gavin stops. "These tunnels were created by Slag. The mountains are riddled with them."

"The dragon? Do you suppose his treasure is in here?"

"Not only do I suppose," he says grimly, "but so must every orc—that's why they're here mining."

You open your mouth, but he presses his hand across your lips. "Listen!"

You can't hear anything, but the two of you edge to the tunnel wall and walk forward cautiously. The tunnel gets lighter. Torches appear to be fixed to the walls up ahead. Also, the tunnel seems to branch out. As you move closer and closer, you can hear the raucous sounds of orcs—drinking and singing, by the noise they're making.

Gavin's nose wrinkles. "Orcs stink," he mutters.

The two of you stop. The tunnel has been going in the direction you wish, though it may now lead to the center of the orcs' barracks. There is a dim chamber opening to your right. You cannot tell if the tunnel will take you to the center of the bawdy celebration, though.

"I don't like the sound of that," Gavin says.

"Me either. Can we get around them?"

"If they're drunk enough. We have your cloak," and he pats his belt, where he secured the cloak before climbing. "But I don't like the risk."

"What about the chamber?" You almost wish you hadn't asked, because you can hear a noise, like someone mumbling or moaning.

"Looks fine to me." Gavin frowns as you tell him you hear something. He listens. "I hear nothing."

How could he, over the noise of the orcs? Also, you know the tunnel goes farther and deeper, but the chamber could merely be a dead end, trapping

37

you at the orcs' mercy. You sigh, afraid to go either way but knowing you must make a decision.

1. If you take the chamber, go to Pathway 58 (page 204).

2. If, thinking you can slip past the boisterous orcs, you keep on, see Pathway 39 (page 146).

PATHWAY
8

As Gavin pulls his sword, you catch his elbow. "Please, let's go around!"

He motions for you to be quiet, then says, "I have an idea." The sun still shines on the mountaintop.

As a hail of gravel is kicked down by the approaching troll, the Ranger stretches his sword at arm's length. As you watch, the blade just catches the sun's glimmer. Gavin moves slightly, and a beam of light glances off the sword. It shoots toward the mountain. Sunlight will kill the monster!

The troll screams in terror and scrambles away.

"That should hold him for a while," Gavin says as he replaces his weapon.

He takes your hand and pulls you up the remaining pathway. You are nearly at the top. Bracken and undergrowth block your path and the two of you use your swords to hack your way through, though it

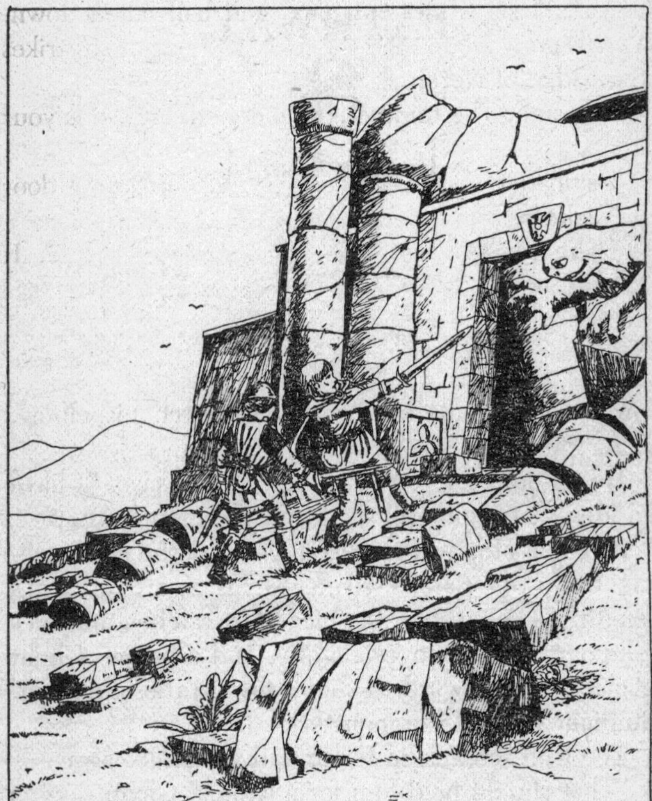

means your blades may be sadly blunted by the time you get free.

At the plateau, the last rays of the sun catch the temple. It is white and pink, and half fallen down. Weeds grow around the columns. Red paint overstrikes the badge of Neron.

You sigh. The temple is abandoned, and so is your hope.

Gavin checks the edge of his weapon. "Front door or back?" he asks simply. "Looks like trouble."

Is he mocking you? Either entry will suffice. It appears to be empty, but you sense an evil aura about the building. Gavin watches you. If you're worried about what may lie inside, the back door may be best. But you're still determined to prove your courage to him, and you are your father's daughter, taught never to be afraid! Which door will you choose?

1. Go to Pathway 42 (page 155) for the back door.
2. Turn to Pathway 36 (page 135) if you choose the front.

PATHWAY 9

"True enough," Gavin agrees. He moves with you to the lighter tunnel, his own hand resting lightly on his sword hilt.

As you move past him to take the lead, he grasps your elbow.

"Mind your step," he says firmly. "I'll follow you every step of the way on this quest of yours, but I want your promise that when it's all over you'll come home with me so that we can get to know each other better."

Your heart leaps in joy as you answer, "I promise, Gavin."

"Good." He releases you so that you can follow the twisting tunnel.

Your footsteps are muffled in the soft dirt. Gavin grows restless as the tunnel turns. "The orc smell is stronger." He scuffs at the floor, which is growing soft and muddy. "The mining work has interfered with the river and lake. We may find ourselves neck-deep in water before we're out of here."

You shudder at the thought, knowing how difficult it is to swim in a mail coat and with weapons. "I hope not!"

The tunnel grows narrower and narrower. Soon you are faced with a cleft that only someone as slim as yourself or Gavin could slip through. You stop in dismay. "Orcs can't possibly have gotten through here!"

"No," says Gavin with satisfaction. "The stink comes from the other side. There's been a cave-in here. They probably can't get through. If we attack, we'll have a definite advantage." He takes your hand. "Now you must decide if you want to go through, or go back and take the blue tunnel."

1. *If you take the cleft, see Pathway 17 (page 69).*
2. *If you double back to the inner blue tunnel, see Pathway 29 (page 115).*

PATHWAY
10

You drop Gavin's hand. "A queen," you say shyly, but give Gavin a wink over your shoulder.

Loric shouts gleefully. He picks you up and throws you over his shoulder like a sack of meal. Your head swims dizzily as he carries you through the caverns.

When he sets you down, you see that he is handsome, in his own way. He takes your hand and kisses it suddenly, kneeling before you. You can't think of a word to say, as you are busily looking around the room for a way out.

Loric's chambers are carved into the rock. Niches hold burning oil lamps. He has a table and chairs, a bookcase filled with odd sorts of treasure he must have looted from the dragon's caves, and a huge bed in one corner.

He stands up. "Share a cup with me . . . on your promise to be my bride."

"Well . . . ah . . . actually, I was thinking of a long engagement. Very long."

"Shy, are you?" he crows, as you back away a little. "I like that in a hussy." He rummages through the bookcase and comes up with a very dusty bottle. "This was from last season, a good year for wine." He takes a tarnished cup down and splashes the burgundy liquid into it. He sits down as you politely refuse a drink.

"Sit, sit."

You remain standing until he shouts and thumps his heavy fist on the table. Then you quickly sit down. Will Gavin never get here? you think.

"Know who I am?"

"Loric, of course," you say, trying to sound as if everyone knows who Loric is, though you have no idea at all.

"That's right! And the kingdom of Rhyll rightfully belongs to me once I can trick my brother out of it. Gold . . . all that lovely gold . . . will buy me an army and a few officials. Soon, I'll be out of here and back where I belong. And you know what I'm gonna do? Take you with me."

"Well, thank you." You look around the dusty room. He appears to have been here awhile. "How long ago did your brother, ah, throw you out?"

"Nicely put." He frowns, trying to remember. "Five years ago last spring. I haven't been here long, though. And soon, I'll have enough gold."

It's clear that he already has enough. You remember Gavin's stories of the curse of dragon gold. Loric's eyes are bloodshot, and his hands tremble violently as you look around at the treasure he has hidden in his room.

"You'll share all this with me?"

"No! That is . . ." He clears his throat, embarrassed. "You can get your own. This is mine, all mine." He stands up from the table. "Give us a kiss, to seal the engagement." He reaches for you.

You think you'd rather have gone down the fearsome tunnel. You sidestep him and grab a chair. The two of you dodge back and forth until you are out of breath and it is only a matter of time until he catches you.

Suddenly, the door blows open in a gust of wind. Loric stops in his tracks, weaving. He gives a drunken sigh and keels over. You drop the chair and sit down, trying to catch your breath.

Gavin appears, the elven cloak draped over his arm. "Just in time, I think."

"Well, you could have come a little sooner!" you snap. One of your braids has come undone. He fingers it lightly.

"Maybe just a little. We'd better hurry. The caravaners are waiting, and now I know the best way out. That's what took me so long!"

You jump up and hug him in delight.

He gently backs away. As you leave, you each take a shining jewel from the bookcase, and a bag of coins, to repay the caravaners for their loss in goods, and because the jewels are quite beautiful.

Ranth grabs you in fierce delight as you hurry to the tunnel to the outside, where they are waiting.

He kisses your hands. "You are wonderful, Sword Daughter! Your father would have been most proud!"

Gavin says fiercely, "We had better leave before Loric wakes."

The caravaners shuffle behind you as Gavin leads the way through the dim tunnel. He is muttering to himself about something, you're not sure what. As you break into the fresh air outside, dawn is tingeing the sky a delicate pink. You didn't know you had been below so long!

Ranth takes his tribesmen and leaves. Gavin faces you, the peaks of the Arad Mountains around you. You are standing on top of the mountain from which the waterfall springs.

"What happened between you and that brute, anyway?"

"Nothing!"

He runs his hand through your loose auburn hair. "Nothing?"

"I promise!"

The jealous look fades from his eyes. "Good!"

You give him a shy look, happy that he was jealous. You say teasingly, "I'm not ready to be anybody's bride—not yet, at least." You blush as he pulls you close in an embrace. "But . . . I'm willing to go home with you and talk about it some more!"

Gavin stills you with a kiss as the morning lights the world about you, a brand-new world full of more wonder than even you had guessed at.

END ADVENTURE

PATHWAY 11

"Can we cross here?" you ask, pointing at the river.

"As good a place as any." Gavin waves your hand away as you offer it to him. "I'll swim across. Two of us may hamper Stormseeker. He'll take you across just fine."

"All right." You press your heels to the horse, urging him to the river. But the creature does not want to enter the water. He paces the muddy bank instead as though looking for something. Despite your cries and many bangs of your heels against his flanks, he trots away from the bank.

"Hold on!" Gavin yells to you as the horse whirls and breaks into a run.

At the last moment, you realize that Stormseeker is going to jump the broad expanse of the Ashkaraneth! You grab his mane tightly and lean over as his muscles bunch. As you gasp in surprise, you are airborne. Then you are down with a thump and the stallion slows to a halt. He snorts and tosses his head up and down as though pleased with himself. You look back. Surely no mortal horse could have done such a feat!

Gavin, holding his weapons over his head, wades into the waters. You watch, holding your breath, as the level rises higher and higher. The normally quiet waters seem to be foaming up now and running quite swiftly. Though his face shows no expression, you fear for Gavin. It is a strange emotion, after all the arguing you have done. But you realize you would be quite alone without him.

Halfway across, the water touches his chin. You watch tensely. Your hands are clenched deep in Stormseeker's mane. Then he is striding out of the water and shaking himself on the bank beside you.

Gavin looks across the Ashkaraneth, frowning. "It is much too low! I should not have been able to walk across."

"What's happening?"

"I don't know, but as the old saying goes, where there are orcs, there is trouble." He dries his sword carefully.

"Orcs are great miners and excavators."

"Yes. Though why that would bother the river . . ." He slaps Stormseeker on the haunches. "Let's hurry and find out." He breaks into a run, and the horse trots after him.

As you travel closer to the Arad Mountains, you find yourself very distracted by Gavin. You say things just to hear his strong, light voice. And you wish you could be running beside him. How foolish your father would think you're being! You almost smile at that.

Gavin points. "The lake! We're nearly there!"

A blue jewel lies sparkling at the base of the mountains. It is huge. You think of taking a luxurious bath when you get there . . . and remind yourself that it will be impossible with orcs nearby. You sigh.

Stormseeker whirls nervously. A cloud of dust approaches. A low rumble, like thunder, can barely be heard.

Gavin pats the horse to quiet him. Then he leans and listens to the ground. He jumps up. "Stampede! They're after the water at the lake!"

Even as he speaks, you can see the herd of wild cattle, their rust-and-cream-colored hides and wickedly curving horns, breaking through the dust cloud. Their lowing and hoofbeats fill the air. They are running at breakneck speed directly toward you!

Gavin turns Stormseeker and slaps him into a run, and strides beside you. As the lake draws nearer, you can see signs of orcish work—a huge wooden structure where the lake spills into the river. They've been trying to dam it! You lean over Stormseeker's neck as the drought-panicked cattle draw nearer and nearer.

Gavin halts. He takes your hand. "Stay on Stormseeker!" He can barely speak, he is so out of breath. "Outrun them! I'll take shelter here!"

He turns and sprints for a jumble of rock and brush sticking up from the hard-baked ground.

You push Stormseeker forward, but look back over

your shoulder. Running with the cattle will be dangerous. Their horns curve long and wickedly to the front, and as they stampede, they are jostling and running blindly. You will be carried far from Gavin and very near to the orcs!

If you jump now, you can reach the same shelter Gavin has taken, just ahead of the thundering herd of wild cattle. Stormseeker will be safe. You hesitate, unsure of what to do, only knowing you do not wish to be alone in orc country.

Bellows split the air! You must decide what you will do quickly!

1. If you urge Stormseeker forward to outrun the stampede, turn to Pathway 50 (page 181).

2. See Pathway 5 (page 23) if you're going to jump and join Gavin.

PATHWAY 12

Knowing that your quest is for honor, you run your hardest. Stormseeker snorts by your side, his silvery mane blowing in the wind. As you stumble again, you reach out to save yourself. Your fingers accidentally grasp his mane. Suddenly, you feel the pulse of his strength. You feel as though you could run forever! The tree looms ahead. Your feet are flying. Gavin is just in front of you now! With a deep breath, you overtake and pass him, just as you reach the tree.

You and Stormseeker slow to a stop, and your hand slips from his neck. The elven horse whickers wisely as you lower your head and take deep breaths. He must have magical powers, for surely you could not have won without him! Gavin walks up slowly, also trying to catch his breath.

"You have won. Though," he continues with an

amused smile, nodding toward the dapple-gray, "you had some help."

"I didn't know!"

"No, you didn't. You won fairly, Tyrna. You have won your right to accompany me." He straightens suddenly. There is a faint noise in the wind which you cannot quite catch.

Stormseeker throws his head up, nostrils flared. Gavin motions for you to be silent. "Trouble! That is a pack of wild dogs, looking for prey." He signals for you to mount Stormseeker. "I don't want us to be dinner!"

The yaps and howls come closer, raising the hairs on the back of your neck. They are hungry and near! You know you can either fight them or try to slip away, hoping they have scented other game. The dogs might scatter if you charge them, however. The two of you hesitate as the howling approaches just on the other side of the ridge of rocks.

1. *If you decide to fight them, turn to Pathway 23 (page 88).*

2. *See Pathway 35 (page 132) if you wish to try to slip away.*

PATHWAY
13

Stormseeker leaps before you even touch a heel to his side, your mind one with his. As the howling whirlwind approaches, grit stings your face and body. But the stallion is too fast for the sand devil.

You lean down as Gavin stands waiting. He grabs your arm and vaults onto the horse's back.

"To water!" he commands.

But the water was a mirage! Puzzled, you give the horse his head. You wrap your hands tightly in Stormseeker's billowing mane as he strains to outrun the sand devil. Its shadow towers over you. Gavin's strong arms grip you about your waist. Though you are both light, your weight slows down the mighty stallion.

Gavin says in your ear, "The riverbed will stop it."

"What river?" you ask, as the wind snatches away your words.

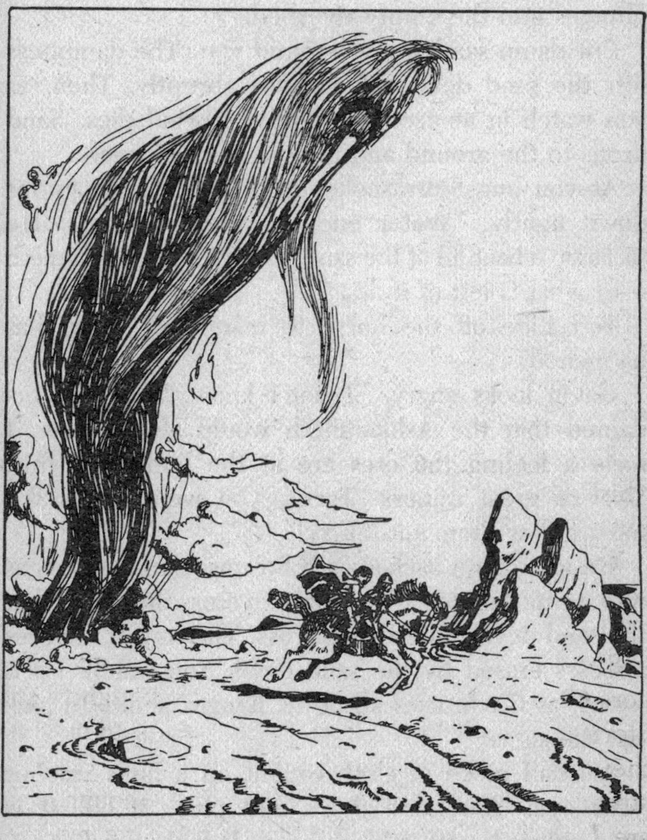

"There!" And he points at the dark, angry trench crossing the wastes in front of you.

"But there's no water!" you protest as Stormseeker plunges into the empty riverbed.

But damp sand sprays around you. The dampness hits the sand devil, which halts abruptly. Then, as you watch in amazement, the whirlwind dies. Sand drops to the ground and the creature is gone!

As you hug Stormseeker in delight, Gavin jumps down lightly. "Water enough," he comments. He picks up a handful of the sand. "This is the Ashkaraneth —or what is left of it."

You slide off the horse to rest him. "What has happened?"

Gavin looks angry. "I don't know. The gods ordained that the Ashkaraneth would always flow. I have a feeling the orcs are at the bottom of this! They're great miners. Tyrna, you were right. We must follow them and hurry!"

He tosses you back aboard Stormseeker and breaks into a run. He doesn't hesitate to cross the waste that the sand devil chased you across. The trail of the orcs appears erased by the sand devil. You watch, fascinated, as Gavin uses all of his Ranger ability to pick out the signs.

A small piece of cloth caught on a bush catches your eye. You bend down and pluck it off. It is sand-colored, with a black band. It looks familiar.

"Look, Gavin! It's part of Ranth's robe—Ranth is the leader of the caravaners!"

"Good. Now we know we're on the right track," says Gavin.

Gavin breaks into a trot. He does not seem to feel tired, but you do. You have been many days in the wasteland heat, using water sparingly all that time. You feel as though you could drink a river.

The Arad Mountains draw close, their cold purple beauty blotting out the distance. Gavin slows and Stormseeker halts. The horse paws the ground. The damp but empty riverbed has appeared again on your left, and you will soon meet with it.

"The orcs came this way." He points to a blue shimmer at the foot of the mountains. "That is the lake—so at least the spring gives out water."

Kneeling on Stormseeker's back, you shade your eyes and study the distant lake. You see the water spilling out upon the desert floor, uselessly flowing into the wilderness. You point out a huge, cruel-looking wooden structure, with timbers cut like spikes.

"That looks like orcish handiwork. Could they have dammed the river?"

"Perhaps. Though why . . .?" Gavin's voice trails off as he looks around. Finally, he says, "The captives were brought through here, there's no doubt of it."

"Then we know where to hit them—right at the watergate."

Gavin shakes his head. "I don't want to risk you or the caravaners. There is the waterfall that empties into the Ashkaraneth from the spring. It leads underground, though I don't know if the passage will lead us around the lake to the orcs. We have a chance to go in quietly if we try it."

You look at the thin spray of the waterfall from the

Arad Mountains. Though it is cool and refreshing, it is far from you, while the dam is close. You know the orcs will be harsh to their prisoners and fear the tribesmen cannot last much longer. You are tired and impatient with all the delays.

"I think we should go in directly," you say.

Gavin looks at you, that strange expression on his face that you saw earlier. Then he looks away. "It is your quest as much as it is mine. I will follow you wherever you go."

1. *Are you determined to go directly to the excavation? See Pathway 52 (page 184).*

2. *Or do you think that Gavin may be right in trying to sneak up on the orcs, though neither of you knows if the underground passage goes through? If so, see Pathway 7 (page 33).*

PATHWAY
14

You lower your sword.

"That's better," Gavin says. "I didn't think you'd killed many orcs."

"You're the Warden here! Do something."

"I intend to," he says grimly, as he hooks his thumbs into his belt. The wind ruffles his sun-gold hair. He is dressed as a Ranger with a bow strapped across his back. His sword is sheathed on his hip. "My duty," he adds slowly, "is to the river first."

"A river!" You can't believe your ears. "Of what use is a river?" you ask, forgetting you would have begged to bathe in it yesterday.

He points across your shoulder. You see the faintest roll of hills to the far south, a touch of green across barren land. The caravaners had warned you and your father away from them, as the high elves live there and the valleys are sacred.

"The Ashkaraneth is our life. Without it, our valleys would be desert like this land."

"Then you are pledged to life. I don't know where to go, but I do know I have to help the caravaners. Let me come with you. Life is short enough without giving in to murdering orcs."

"I don't intend to give in to them."

You take your elven cloak from his hand. "I'm not only my father's daughter, but his pupil, his Sword Daughter. I must avenge his death."

"You'll have to do it with me, then, because I don't intend to leave you out here alone. We'll travel the Ashkaraneth, then circle and trail the orcs."

"But the caravaners!"

He shakes his head. "They are a hardy people . . . let's hope they can wait. But the river brings life to many, and I have to go there first."

He turns and whistles. A beautiful horse, white with dapple-gray clouds upon him, appears from behind the rocks. The creature whinnies softly and eyes you. You know immediately that he is a prince of horses, a swift and intelligent mount.

Gavin bends to give you a leg up. "You ride and I will run beside you."

"But—"

The Ranger frowns at you. "No more buts will I allow you! We've got to leave before the orcs double back. The two of us will tire Stormseeker too quickly. We have a long way to travel."

"Then you ride, and I will run," you say proudly. You brace yourself for his answer. "I'm in condition."

"You were hit on the head."

"I have a tough head."

"You'll have no head at all if you stand here in the hot sun and argue with me!" Gavin breaks off angrily. You have succeeded in breaking legendary elven calm. "You ride for a while, and then I will," he says quietly. "Fair enough?"

You let him toss you lightly aboard his horse. Though you did not really want to do any running just yet, you wanted to prove to him that you can hold your own. You have a feeling he has no intention of letting you go after the orcs, now or later. You will have to change his mind along the way.

As you leave the bloody battlefield, you don't look back. You cannot even give your father a burial, for if the orcs return, everything must be the same. But you know he would have understood, for he was an understanding father as well as a great general.

Gavin runs alongside you. He is strong and tireless, though the ground is rocky as well as sandy. The hot sun does not seem to bother him. You watch him more than you care to admit, having not seen a lot of young men, but liking to watch him. The leagues pass away quickly beneath the strides of the elven horse and the Ranger.

Gavin signals you to stop. "The river is close."

"I can't see anything."

He unslings the water bag from his belt as he says, "It is there, nonetheless." He waits as though expecting you to argue. Then he offers you a drink from the bag.

You swallow sweet, almost bubbly water. It quenches your thirst, yet you cannot quite remember what it tasted like after you hand the water bag back. Is this Ashkaraneth magical water?

Stormseeker whickers anxiously. Gavin silences you and listens with his keen, elven senses.

"Wild dogs," he says finally. He kneels and puts his ear to the ground. "A large pack, and they're looking for dinner. I don't want it to be us!"

The faint yap and howl of the pack reaches you. You have few enough arrows and don't feel like shooting an animal that is only doing what it has to do to survive. You hope that Gavin has the skill to guide you away from them. On the other hand, if you charge into the pack, you may frighten them enough to scatter them. The barking grows close. Gavin hesitates. You must decide what action to urge him into.

1. *If you wish to slip past the wild dogs, turn to Pathway 35 (page 132).*

2. *If you wish to urge Gavin into a direct attack, in hopes of scaring the dogs off, turn to Pathway 23 (page 88).*

PATHWAY
15

"I won't beg you," you say and turn away. You aren't very good at tears anyway, and you don't think Gavin would listen. But you've an idea and look up immediately. "Test me."

"What?"

"Test me! If I'm not good enough, then I'll go to your valley. But if I can prove I can keep up with you, take me with you!"

Lips curved in an amused smile, Gavin says, "All right then. Wits as well as skill, agreed? I'll pick one trial and you the other."

You agree, wondering if you've done the right thing as he says, "I pick a footrace, you against me."

You groan. "That's not fair! You're an elf. I can't possibly keep up with you."

"You wished a test," he reminds you, one eyebrow rising. "Besides, I'm only half elven. If you want to keep up with me, you'll have to prove it. And your choice of trials?"

You think quickly. "A riddle contest. I'll ask, you answer—and if you can't, I win." This contest is a little one-sided, too, for elves have little knowledge of human humor, but you have to do something to offset the race!

"Fair enough." Gavin folds his arms and looks down in amusement. "Riddle away!"

You think quickly of a favorite your father taught you. "Okay. Listen carefully: Two legs sits on three legs holding one leg. Up jumps four legs and steals one leg. Two legs throws three legs after four legs which drops one leg. What has happened?"

Stormseeker appears to whicker in approval and paws the ground. You gently warn the creature, "No fair telling him!"

Long moments go by as Gavin thinks. A tiny wrinkle appears between his eyes as he frowns. Finally he says, "I give up."

You smile in triumph as you tell him, "A man sits down on a three-legged stool to eat his leg of mutton. His dog jumps up and steals the mutton. The man throws his stool at the dog, which, scared, drops the mutton and runs off!"

Stormseeker gives a horse laugh, and even Gavin laughs at himself. "That's a good one, Tyrna! I must remember that—giants love a good riddle. All right, you've wit enough, but are you fast enough? To that far tree, and you must keep up with me or pass me to win! Are you ready?"

You don't feel anything of the sort, but you must abide by your own rules. You nod.

"Go!" Gavin shouts, and the two of you sprint away. The ground is broken and uneven, rocks and brush thrusting out of nowhere. The Ranger draws away tirelessly, his feet barely touching the ground.

Stormseeker paces you as you race in hot pursuit. But you watch in dismay. It seems impossible to catch up with Gavin, and you must continue your quest! You stumble and nearly fall. It gives you an idea. If you call out you have fallen, Gavin will return for you. You can cheat, passing him then.

You pant, not wanting to think of cheating, though you guess it couldn't really be called cheating, just using your wits again. You're fast, and you might be able to catch up. Gavin seems to be slowing. You are desperate as the tree draws closer. You don't want to be left behind and sent to the valleys. You take a deep breath and run faster, wondering what you should do—cheat and cry out, or try your hardest to win fairly.

1. *If you decide to cry out, go to Pathway 48 (page 176).*

2. *Turn to Pathway 12 (page 52) if you wish to try to win fairly.*

PATHWAY 16

You say in a rather small voice, "I'd really like to go home with you."

Gavin grabs you in a fierce hug, saying nothing, but you can feel the joy in his embrace. He lets you go. "You're sure?"

You nod. He leads you across the sands, out of sight of the dam, and whistles for Stormseeker. The stallion returns and prances in front of the two of you, his muzzle wet with water from the lake.

Gavin laughs and rubs the horse's neck. He then grasps you about the waist and lightly tosses you aboard. He mounts behind you, wrapping one strong arm about your waist to keep you steady. "Home," he commands.

With a playful rear, Stormseeker breaks into a gentle lope, the ground flying away beneath his hooves.

Gavin squeezes you about the waist. His mouth is near your ear as he says, "You'll like the valley. It's quiet and peaceful. You can stay with my mother. She'll take care of you, because I need to be gone a lot. She must be the best bread baker around."

"She bakes bread?" you ask, knowing that you can't.

"So light, and the crust is always chewy," Gavin answers wistfully. "You can bake, can't you?"

"No . . . not really. I never had time for it. I was always helping my father."

"Oh. Well, she'll teach you. I'll bet you're good with kids, though."

You are beginning to wonder what he wishes of you. "Okay, I guess, as long as they mind and leave me alone."

Gavin laughs heartily. "Leave you alone! That's funny, Tyrna! I hope we have lots of children. I love them."

Your heart sinks in dismay. You're too young to think of children! You haven't done enough growing up yourself yet—and what about all the great things you'd like to do? Children don't fit into your ideas of fun right now.

"Gavin," you start hesitantly, but he interrupts you.

"Oh, don't worry, Tyrna. I don't think we should start right away. After all, you're hardly more than a child yourself. You can help my mother around the house, and when you're a little older, we can have the betrothal party and—well, the rest will just fall into place as you mature."

Mature! You were on your way to the Warrior Games, to take your place in formal training as a fighter. You dream of adventure and glory. Who does he think you are? You sigh as he tightens his arms about you. You had hoped for an elven courtship—magical places to go and things to do. Instead, he intends to shut you away with his mother while you learn to do housekeeping. Ugh!

Wondering if you haven't made a serious mistake, you realize your only hope is that you will meet someone a little more romantic in the valleys, or maybe sneak off to join a caravan that will take you onto the Warrior Games, where you can find a more exciting future.

END ADVENTURE

PATHWAY
17

"Through here," you say, squeezing through quickly. Gavin follows. Silence draws around both of you as you face a great, dimly lit hall.

Candlelight illuminates heaps of treasure piled haphazardly around. As you reach for a beautiful object, Gavin grasps your hand.

"Don't touch it, Tyrna! Dragon gold carries the curse of the dragon that gathered it. It looks beautiful, but it's deadly."

Reluctantly, you move away from the sparkling emerald ring. "But I've heard of fortunes being won from a dragon. It can't all be bad."

"Strong sunlight will cleanse it."

With a sigh, you follow him across the empty hall. It opens onto a corridor. Gavin strides through eagerly, pointing out the main excavation works.

"Look! The caravaners!"

Ranth and his tribesmen are seated wearily, their backs to the great watergate that dams the Ashkaraneth. Mining tools are scattered all around. Their robes are covered with dirt and mud, and their hands are raw. You saw away their bonds. Beyond, you can hear the sound of orcs drinking and gaming.

Ranth bows his head over your hands as you cut him loose. "Praise be, praise be. You must beware Ashkaran!"

"Ashkaran?" you ask, as you quickly free the others. They are dazed and fearfully repeat the word.

"Ashkaran is the caravaner name for the blue dragon Slag."

Ranth clasps your hands again. "He lives! He is trapped here, underground! After we finish the last tunnel, we are to be fed to him!"

Gavin curses, then looks at you. "I'm sorry, Tyrna. But these greedy orcs may free the dragon in their eagerness to get all the gold!"

"That's terrible."

Ranth pulls you away. "Come quickly—let me guide you out!"

You and Gavin stare toward the tunnel concealing the orcs. You both have the same thought, but Gavin quickly sheathes his dagger. "Tomorrow we'll settle with them," he tells you. "And the dragon must be dealt with, once and for all. Tonight, I'll see you home."

With Ranth hurrying you, you flee through the tunnels into the darkness. As the caravaners scatter, eager to reach the mountains before the orcs know they are gone, Gavin whistles up Stormseeker.

As you wait in the darkness for the magnificent stallion to answer his call, you think of all that has happened. You're both sad and happy.

"Gavin," you say softly, as you put your hand into his. "Take me back with you, so that I can finish my quest. Somewhere down there is the orc that killed my father."

He places his warm hand over yours. "Done, but only if you let me guard that fiery temper of yours, because I don't intend to lose you now that I've found you."

"Agreed," you answer, and the two of you seal the bargain with a kiss in the soft summer night.

END ADVENTURE

PATHWAY 18

"We must fight!" Gavin declares. He draws his long sword and motions for you to do the same.

As the hail of rocks and gravel nearly consumes you, you pull yourselves up to the knoll. You hold your weapon ready. Any battle with the troll will be a dread one, as the slimy monster can heal itself almost as fast as it can be injured. Only fire will stop the beast! As night falls across the mountain, you can see its shambling gray shape. It is horrible, with dangling arms and a huge evil grin.

It swipes at you. You leap aside and swing, but the sword blow merely glances off its stonelike hide. It will be a terrible fight!

Gavin raises his weapon to strike, but suddenly torchlight surrounds you.

With a moan, the troll scrambles back to its nest.

As brigands and orcs ring you, holding their torches high, a cleric comes forward.

He folds his arms in delight, saying to his men, "My pretty is better than a watchdog, is it not?"

In the flickering light, the cleric looks as evil as the troll! His robes are decorated with foul symbols. He strokes his pointed beard and motions for his followers to guide you up the slopes. Gavin holds your hand tightly. The gesture doesn't make you feel much better as you whisper to him, "I don't like this."

"Neither do I," the Ranger answers.

The temple of Neron looms from the darkness, its white pillars and roof gleaming. Your heart plunges as you see the terrible symbols of black sorcery painted over its surface. Evil has struck down the very help you sought. The cleric pauses at the front entrance.

"My name is Kolroth. Welcome to my sanctuary."

"This was once Neron's," you say angrily.

"Once, but no more." He smiles, a mean gesture, as you are forced inside by his followers.

The torches are put into their holders, and he motions for his men to leave. "I wish to talk to them privately." He strokes his oily beard as they obey.

The three of you study each other. At the rear of the temple, a huge statue in tribute to Neron looks down. Shadows seem to give it a sad expression. You continue to hold tightly to Gavin for comfort.

"I am pleased you have come. The caravaners my orcs brought didn't last the trip. I need a sacrifice for the full of the moon. You two will do nicely!"

You shudder in horror. Your voice is stuck in your

throat with fear and you cannot answer, but Gavin lunges forward. "Never!" he shouts defiantly.

Kolroth's men instantly appear, jumping him. "Run, Tyrna!" he commands you, as you stand free.

Indecision stops you. The troll lurks outside in the darkness—and you don't want to leave Gavin alone! You have a desperate idea as you look around the temple of Neron. Surely some of that paladin's favor with the gods remains, some spark of goodness. Should you try to summon Neron's aid, or run and leave Gavin to struggle alone?

1. If you try to summon the ancient powers, see Pathway 21 (page 84).

2. But if you obey Gavin and leave him, turn to Pathway 49 (page 179).

PATHWAY 19

You put your hands in the air to show the orcs you will not fight any longer, hoping they will take you captive as they did the caravaners.

Torg shoves you in the back. "Narr. Cowardly fighter. Orcs fight good!" But he takes your weapons.

As you stumble, your helmet falls off and your braids come tumbling down. The orcs jump back in surprise.

"Long hair!"

Torg edges close, his nasty eyes narrowed. Then he grabs one of your braids and hoists it high in the air, nearly pulling you off the ground with it. Your scalp hurts as he yells, "This woman! I think good idea make present to Loric!"

"No!" you cry, but it's too late as he scoops you up, slings you over his shoulder, and takes off at a run.

The bump and jostle makes your head throb, and you black out.

Oof! You come to as the orc drops you on a hard dirt surface. Your hands are tied and throb in pain. You sit up, seeing that there are dirt walls all around you. You are underground in a cave or tunnel. Torches light the dimness. Ahead of you, the tunnel opens into a large chamber, and you can see a wicked-looking wooden structure, with logs like battering rams tied together. It must be what stems the flow of the river! There are mining tools and barrels for hauling dirt scattered all over the place. The orcs might be good miners, you think, but they certainly are sloppy ones.

A hearty laugh fills the air behind you.

You scramble to your feet, as a big hand helps you to stand. You look up—and up—into a rugged, but handsome face half hidden by a curly black beard. This must be Loric the fighter!

"I be Loric, warlord," he says, his deep voice rumbling. "Who are you, with your flame-colored hair?"

Your voice sticks in your throat. You are both attracted and repelled by the man in front of you. He crosses his powerful arms across his chest as he waits for your answer. "I'm Tyrna," you answer weakly.

Without a reply, he reaches out and loosens your braids, so that your hair lies free across your shoulders. "Thank you, Torg," he says without turning to the orc leader behind him. "She's a pretty prize!" He draws his dagger and cuts your bonds loose.

Your wrists sting as the blood rushes through them,

and you stand, rubbing them. You eye Loric. He has no idea of your training. You might be able to surprise him and get away yet.

Loric says to Torg, "My men tell me you were busy yesterday."

The orc bares his long teeth in a horrible grin. "We took slaves! Good help in new tunnels. They brought along a big sword, but Torg took care of him!"

Loric scratches his chin. "Watch it, Torg. We don't want any trouble until we're ready for it! It's going to take more gold to buy a big enough army for conquering."

Greedy laughter fills the cavern, and your heart strains near to breaking at the thought of your father.

Loric takes you by the elbow. "Come, my pretty. I wouldn't want you getting lost down here!"

You go reluctantly. There is no sight of the caravaners, but the caves and tunnels are really quite beautiful. Rocks like icicles hang from the ceilings, in all colors of the rainbow. Crystals lie open in the walls, their snowflake beauty shining in the torchlight. But you stop in astonishment as Loric shows you a chamber, for here lies not only the treasures of the earth but vast treasures of man, too! They have found the dragon hoard of Slag's End!

"This will buy my kingdom back!" says Loric triumphantly. He waves a hand over the treasures, coins, vases, jewels, swords, crowns, statues—everything imaginable. Gold and silver and pearls and emeralds and rubies glitter in the torchlight. "Merkle, evil warlord, overran my brothers and took our lands. It has taken me a few years to gather mercenaries like myself—mean enough and tough enough to take it back! This treasure will buy more, until I can be sure of victory!"

You feel sorry for him, but you say, "Taking slaves and killing others is no way to do it!"

"What do you know, eh?" he sneers. "Power is what counts, girl. Never forget it. Power and gold."

You shrug and bend over, picking up a coin. He strikes it from your hand.

"It's mine! All mine! You may never touch it!" Loric cries, an evil and crazed look in his eyes.

You shrink back against the cave wall, knowing that the treasure has cursed him with its evil and greed.

Loric looks ashamed. "I'm sorry." He strokes your hair. "You remind me of my sister—may Merkle die for hurting her! I will free my people yet!"

"Is that what you really wish?"

He looks deeply into your eyes. "Yes," he says and looks away, a tear at the corner of his eye. You are touched. He digs out a coronet. The clink and jingle of coins attracts you.

You feel your eyes drawn to the dragon gold. It begins to sing inside your head, telling you how beautiful it is. You try not to listen or look at it, but you can't tear your eyes away!

Loric holds the coronet out. "Be my queen, fiery beauty!"

"No—I can't!" you stammer. The sight of the treasure inflames you. Loric places the coronet on your hair. It is cold and hard, but instantly power fills you. You know it is the curse and that you must not give in! On the other hand, Loric's tale is sad. With your help, he could become good again and regain his lands. He is not totally lost yet, and you do find him handsome. You struggle to remember who you really are. Will you give in to the temptation or will you fight it?

1. If you think you can be yourself and still be Loric's queen, see Pathway 51 (page 183).

2. If you fight, turn to Pathway 55 (page 194).

PATHWAY
20

Gavin grabs your hand and pulls you forward. "We're in no condition to fight!" he says, as he dives behind a pile of coins, pulling you with him.

A lightning bolt sizzles the air overhead. Gavin motions for you to crawl forward with him. Your heart pounding in your ears, as Slag rattles his chains and roars with spite, you follow.

Dragon gold glows all around you. You swallow, remembering Gavin's caution not to retrieve any. Thoughts of the fortune you once wanted fill your head. Now you would give anything to be safe and free with Gavin!

"Come back, little stings!" Slag entreats you. Another lightning bolt stabs the ground in front of you. Its force knocks you on your back, stunned.

Gavin picks you up tenderly as your ears ring. "Are you all right?"

"Yes, I—I think so. That was too close!"

He points toward an exit yawning in the blue crystal cavern. "Through there—it's the nearest!"

"What are you going to do?"

"Play target—now go!" And he pushes you ahead.

You run out of the cavern, coins slipping and skittering beneath your boots. You are trampling a king's ransom as you run! Gavin is at your back, as thunder and lightning shake the ground once again.

The chamber you enter is alive with torchlight! You stop in awe. Even more treasure is here, piled up so thickly you can scarcely walk through it. Gavin gives a low whistle.

"And if I know dragons," he says, "we still haven't reached his main lair. Slag's favorite treasures will be hoarded there, along with his nest and any young he may have."

"Young?"

The half-elven Ranger shrugs. "Even dragons have babies. Though I doubt Slag has had the opportunity."

You pick up a pretty but plain-looking bottle. It is stoppered with cork and sealed. "What do you suppose this is?"

"Drop it!" a crazed voice commands.

The two of you freeze, as a figure walks from behind the heaps of cursed treasure. It is a cleric, stroking his pointed beard.

"So you two escaped Slag, eh? Your caravaner friends weren't so lucky!" the man says.

Though you rarely judge a person by his looks, this man is clearly evil. It gives you the chills just to look at him. He looks at the bottle in your hands and gives a frantic yell.

"You found it! Give it to me! Only I, Kolroth, am great enough to know what to do with it! Give it here!"

Gavin pulls you aside. "He's dabbling in the black arts—look at his robes and tattoos. Whatever is in that bottle is bound to be evil!" He raises his voice, saying to the cleric, "Perhaps we can trade it for a way out."

Kolroth looks sly. "Only three ways out of here. Back the way you came, into the dragon's jaws! Or into that tunnel there, the dark and damp opening into the depths of the earth. Or"—and he points—"back into the center of the mountain, to the wellhead of the Ashkaraneth! Come with me, and I'll show you the underground spring from which the mighty lake is born! You'll be safest there."

"Not the spring," Gavin mutters. "He is bound to have been the one who tampered with it and has the orcs about mining. He probably has more guards there!"

"Speak up!" snaps the cleric irritably. "It's rude to whisper!"

As Gavin turns to you, Kolroth suddenly springs across the chamber. Gavin cries in pain and dismay as he falls beneath the attack. As the cleric stumbles to his feet and charges for you, Gavin yells, "I'm all right, Tyrna! Run for it!"

You are faced with fighting the cleric yourself or taking the tunnel Kolroth seemed to be afraid of. Going back to Slag is out of the question—and you agree with Gavin that the cleric is not to be trusted; you don't want to go the way he has suggested. You have the bottle, full of whatever evil Kolroth seeks. What will you do?

1. *If you take the dank tunnel, turn to Pathway 54 (page 191).*
2. *If you decide to stand and fight Kolroth, go to Pathway 57 (page 201).*

PATHWAY 21

"I'm here, Gavin!" you pledge even as Kolroth strikes his wooden staff on the temple floor.

Gavin, caught on all sides by Kolroth's men, collapses suddenly.

The evil cleric laughs. "You're in my power now!" he tells you.

"No!" You wrestle your sword loose from the brigand who tries to grasp you. You raise it to the temple roof. "By the powers that guided Neron and my father Hamroth, I call for aid! Help us now in the name of good and justice!"

Kolroth halts in fear. A creaking noise fills the temple. The brigands and orcs fall back in confusion, leaving Gavin. With a groan and a moan, the huge stone statue of Neron begins to move!

You help Gavin to stand as Kolroth freezes in astonishment. "Come back!" he shouts uselessly at his followers. They flee in terror from the giant statue as it lumbers across the temple floor, moving faster and faster.

Kolroth points his staff and shouts horrible words at the statue. It begins to crack and topple—and crashes down directly on the evil cleric.

Gavin grabs your arm. "We've got to run!" he shouts, as the entire building begins to sway.

The two of you rush out as it caves into dust, burying Kolroth and his evil for all time. The brigands and orcs have gone.

Gavin takes you into his arms. "You stayed for me!" he says fiercely. "That was a brave thing to do."

"Brave and stupid!"

He takes your chin in his hands, so that you must look into his eyes. "People do such things when they're in love." As you protest, he stills your words with a gentle kiss. "Come home with me."

You answer by returning his kiss.

END ADVENTURE

PATHWAY 22

With a yell, you kick your heels into Stormseeker. You charge through the rocks at the sand devil. Stormseeker fights your command as you draw your sword. Your throbbing headache disappears. Gavin shouts at you in anger, the horse shies away, and you lose your balance.

You fall and twist in midair, landing on your feet, sword ready. Wind and sand whip your face as the sand devil nears you.

You swing at the vortex. It shrieks and twists, and as you dance away, you see you have done absolutely no damage. It blots out the sky above you. What is this beast? Nothing but wind and gravel?

It howls. You swear that an arm buffets you as it approaches. You sense fear and hunger. The fear is yours and the hunger is its! This is no opponent you can face in the arena—you don't even know if it's alive or not!

You continue to dance and slash at it.

Gavin yells, "Hang on, Tyrna, I'm coming!"

As you parry and thrust at an impossible enemy, you pray that Gavin knows how to defeat it. You hope as Gavin approaches that the two of you will survive.

But Gavin stumbles as he tries to circle the force. As he falls, he is slurped up in a hail of gravel. One second he is there, the next he is not.

Grimly, you tighten your hands on your sword hilt and prepare for your last stand, knowing that the sand devil will not let you go.

END ADVENTURE

PATHWAY 23

"We can scare them off if we charge them," you say.

He shakes his head. "If the river has been low, game may have left the area—they could be very hungry!" He motions for you to lower your bow, as he pulls his sword. You follow suit.

The wild dogs top the butte in front of you. Their eyes are frantic, their jaws gaping open with their eager howls. The chilling sounds frighten you. Their ears are pointed, their tails long and furry; they look much like wolves, though they are gray-and-dun-colored, like the wastelands. Their fangs glisten.

You remember that your father taught you the best defense is a good offense—and with a shout, you dig your heels into Stormseeker and charge the beasts! Gavin yells in dismay.

The stallion gallops right at the dogs, as they snap

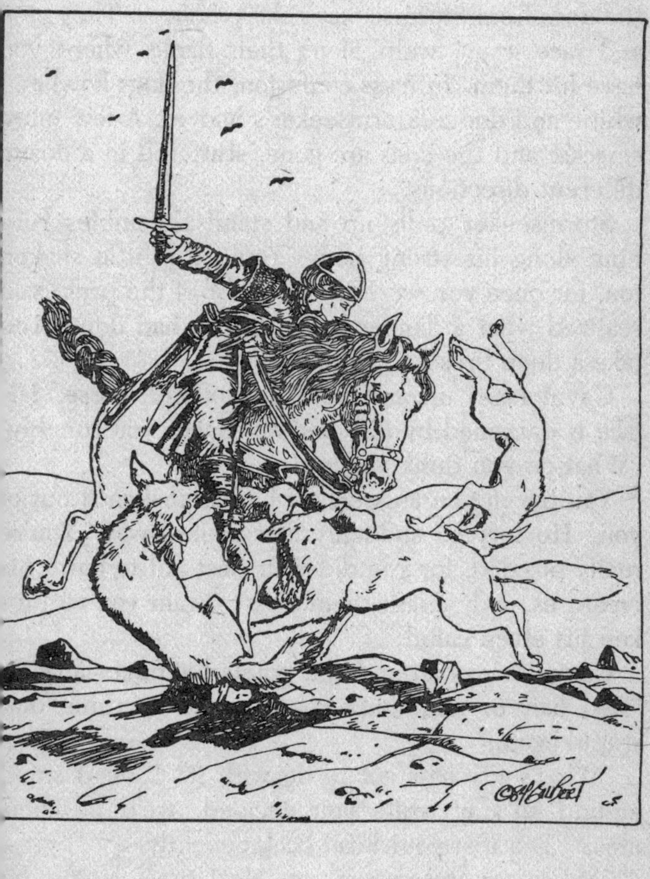

and leap at his graceful legs. He kicks and whirls, nearly unseating you. You lean down and use the flat of your sword blade. Whap! Whap! Your blade smacks the dogs from Stormseeker's sharp hooves. They yelp and race away, welts along their flanks where you have hit them. In mass confusion, the dogs howl and whine and dodge Stormseeker's hooves. A few more smacks, and the dogs are gone, scattered in a dozen different directions.

Stormseeker pulls up and stands, trembles running along his strong body. You are a little shaken too, for once you were in the midst of the pack, you realized what a dangerous thing you had done! You take a deep breath.

Gavin races up and pulls you off the horse. His face is darkened by fury and he shakes you roughly. "What do you think you're doing?"

You haven't an answer, for he has shaken it out of you. He lets go suddenly and stalks away. You're really puzzled, for you did your best not to harm his creatures, only chase them away. Again you've broken his elven calm!

Gavin swings around and points his finger at you. "Red hair or not, don't you ever do anything that stupid again!"

"What's my hair got to do with it? If we'd stood around all day while you decided, we'd be their meal!" You toss your head back defiantly.

"Maybe so and maybe not. Next time, let me be the judge. Your hotheadedness is going to get us both into trouble. Now mount up, and let's get out of here before they decide to come back!"

You have your feet planted firmly on the ground. Gavin takes one look at your face and picks you up by the waist and sets you firmly down on Stormseeker's back. "No more arguing! You'll do as I say," he finishes and strides off, the stallion following.

You travel in silence, the back of Gavin's neck all you can see of the Ranger. You're really puzzled by his anger . . . it's almost as if he really cared for you. After all, your father used to act like that once in a while. But you don't have much time to think about it, as you keep your hands wrapped in Stormseeker's silken mane and the ground passes below you.

Suddenly, you see a streak of the purest blue across the horizon. You point it out, asking, "What's that?"

"The river," Gavin answers without turning.

As you draw closer, the air seems cooler and fresher. Soon, you are standing on the riverbank while Gavin surveys the area. The river is wide, but seems shallow. It is flat and calm and a deep, beautiful color, but is doing absolutely nothing. It does not even seem to be running swiftly. You are a little disappointed. So this is the mighty Ashkaraneth!

"Too low," he mutters, kicking at the damp riverbank. "And look here." He runs his fingers over very strange-looking tracks. "We don't want to meet him out here!"

You don't know who "him" is, but from the looks of the monstrous tracks, you agree.

A worried frown on his face, Gavin pulls a boat out from overhanging shrubs. He looks at you. "We can cross here, and ride up to the lake, or we can go by boat."

"It's upstream!"

He smiles. "We'll have to pole it. But it may be safer. Some of the creatures around here either cannot or will not cross running water."

You're so tired you can hardly hold your head up. You don't feel like poling any boat anywhere. Stormseeker's back would be a welcome rest. And, as he proved during the bout with the wild dogs, his sharp hooves would be a real help if your path should cross the marauding orcs'. Gavin waits to see what you wish to do.

1. *If you agree that boating may be safer, turn to Pathway 2 (page 14).*

2. *See Pathway 11 (page 48) if you wish to continue riding.*

PATHWAY 24

You back down as Gavin holds your hand. He follows, the two of you slipping and sliding in your haste. The bandages rip from your hands. But the moaning and grunts of the troll follow you down.

"It's coming after us," you say in fear. Gavin is above you.

"Hurry," he calls back, and you let your body slide down the mountainside in clumsy haste.

As you jump to the ground, Gavin still clings to the mountain. You see the troll in the shadows for the first time. You stifle a scream. It is monstrously ugly, with long dangling arms and a slimy gray body. Its mouth is a fanged slit in its flat face. Only fire can defeat a troll, for it heals itself almost quicker than a fighter can injure it. Gavin tosses his pack to you.

"There's a flint in it!" he calls anxiously. As you scramble through the pack's contents, Stormseeker gallops in from the lakeside. He neighs in fury as the troll gives a wicked laugh and swings at Gavin with its clawed hand.

The Ranger narrowly dodges the troll, his shirt tearing. Stormseeker rears and strikes at the beast with his hooves. The troll merely grins. It loves horseflesh to eat as much as it does elf or human!

The pack falls to the ground, contents slipping. You drop to your knees, searching wildly in the twilight to find the flint—fire is your only hope. As you look up, the troll has Gavin cornered. His sword is out and he is swinging with all his might, but cannot really hurt the troll. Stormseeker rears again, but Gavin has his back to the mountain as the troll closes in!

Desperately, you grab the water bag and throw it at the back of the troll's head. It splits, and the magical waters of the Ashkaraneth pour over the beast. To your amazement, the monster turns instantly to stone!

Gavin lowers his sword with a sigh of relief. "Tyrna!" he cries happily as you race to his side and hug him.

As the two of you embrace, there are muffled cries from the mountain. You stop. "What's that?"

"I don't know." Sheathing his weapon, Gavin begins to climb up again. You follow, and this time it is easier. As you reach the evil-smelling den of the stone troll, the cries become louder.

Gavin lights a torch and hands it to you so that you can see. As the two of you enter the den, you see the caravaners, trussed like pigs in a market, hanging from the cave's ceiling.

Ranth struggles against his gags and bonds. Gavin cuts him down. Your torchlight strikes the rear of the cave, revealing heaps of treasure! The caravaner hugs you in gratitude.

"The orcs brought us here. They know the troll's den leads down into the lair of the old dragon—they thought if it was kept well fed, they could loot the dragon treasure! Bless you and praise you! I thought we were all dead!"

As Gavin cuts the last caravaner free, he says, "You nearly were. Tyrna saved me, for the troll had me cornered." As he puts his dagger aside, he bends over the treasure the troll has dragged up. "Pick out whatever you want." He takes a beautiful coronet and places it over your long hair. "I suggest this one."

With joy and happiness, you spend the night choosing your fortune from the dead troll's hoard. In the morning, the caravaners go their way. But you no longer have a destination—the Warrior Games seem very far away and unimportant now. You have avenged your father by saving the caravaners, and discovered that it is not nearly as glorious to be a fighter as you thought. You have other emotions on your mind now.

As the rising sun greets you and Gavin, you face each other shyly. You hardly know what to say to him.

"Gavin . . . would you take me home to see your elven valleys? I—I've always wanted to see an elf kingdom. They're supposed to be wonderful!" You hold your breath, hoping he doesn't say no or think you're being silly.

But great joy lights his face as he embraces you. "Yes! But they'll be even more wonderful now that I have you!"

END ADVENTURE

PATHWAY
25

"Gavin!" you cry frantically, trying to pull loose from Loric. "Help me!"

With a shout, Gavin throws off the brigand cloak. The tunnel lightens with a white-hot flare ringing his elven form as he draws his sword. The orcs howl and gnash their teeth, afraid to charge him. Loric lets go of you suddenly as he fumbles for his weapon.

You run to Gavin's side. He pushes you behind him. His voice rings out in a language you don't know, and the very walls of the cave seem to tremble. The orcs charging nearby throw themselves to the floor and cover their ears. Loric turns pale and stops in his tracks.

Gavin turns. "Let's go!" He takes your elbow and the two of you dodge into the fearsome blue tunnel.

The tunnel floor darts downward until you are running so fast you don't know if you can keep your feet. Suddenly, the floor is slick and you fall, your body sliding down the tunnel. Gavin joins you.

The two of you tumble down the slide. Suddenly the tunnel opens up and you are falling through the air. You land with a clash and jingle in a heap of gold, coins flying everywhere. Gavin thumps beside you unceremoniously.

You stop and look around. You're in an immense underground cavern! It looks as though you are below the lake, for the ceiling is crystal and the blue light filtering down from above shimmers as though through water.

Gavin gasps and grabs your arm. You twist backward—and see the snout of a blue dragon behind you!

Gavin puts a hand over your mouth just in time to muffle your scream. As you catch your breath, he whispers in your ear, "He's asleep—and chained."

The two of you very cautiously back off the hill of gold. Then you peer around curiously at the beast. Its hide is also a sapphire blue. It is big, though not as big as some dragons get. It is chained by each leg to a tall pillar that holds up the crystal roof of the cavern.

Gavin says quietly, "That must be Slag! So, he lives yet—but in eternal torment. If he moves but a hair too much, he'll bring the roof down on his head!"

"How do we get out of here?" You are so frightened you can barely talk.

Gavin smiles. "There must be a dozen or more

entrances and exits. We'll just look around and find one."

Still whispering, the two of you cautiously begin to scout around the cavern. You check a few chambers hopefully, only to find dead ends. Gavin starts to leave your side, but you grab his elbow fearfully. The sleeping dragon gives you the creeps.

"Don't leave me alone!"

"We've got to find a way out."

A third voice interrupts, a honeyed voice, dry with amusement. "I wouldn't bother if I were you, little worm. There's only one other exit, and I took great care to hide it well."

The two of you freeze in your tracks as Slag's eyes open and he lifts his magnificent head. He stretches forth a claw and beckons with it.

"Come closer, noisy little worms. Don't worry about me—I had quite a nice dinner. I shan't be hungry for some time. But I am bored. Come play with me, little mouses—or I shall blast you!"

Gavin shoves you behind him and faces the dragon. You warn him, "Don't look in his eyes!" But the Ranger has already taken care.

"What dinner?" he demands boldly.

Slag tilts his head. With a laughing hiss, he indicates the pile of bones and robes at his feet. You give a small cry as you recognize the colorful robes of the caravaners. You came too late!

You hide your face from the sight. Gavin shifts and seems to grow taller. "Tell me the way out!"

"Or you'll loose your elven powers on me? Oh,

yes, I heard the echoes of your war cry. It works well with the craven, but I am Slag! You are powerless here, mortal . . . and it's only a matter of time before the curse of the treasure flames your blood . . . or I grow hungry again. What does it matter if you play a little game with me first?"

"I'll play—if you let her go!"

"Ahhh." The dragon seems to draw itself up. Suddenly it lunges, the chains rattle, and it lashes out. Gavin is thrown to one side as you feel the dragon clutching your body and you are lifted into the air!

You try to scream, but your whole body is paralyzed. You twist your head so that you can't see into the dragon's eyes. Gavin staggers to his feet.

Slag remarks, "My chains are longer than they look. Not much, but enough! Tell me . . . are you the ones responsible for my missing coins? A drabble here, a dribble there? You're a human! I know their fondness for my wealth. I want it returned!"

"No!" Gavin shouts. "We didn't take it! But I know who did. Put her down, and I'll tell you."

"In trade for a way out?" The dragon laughs. "I appear to be in a better bargaining position than you."

"Not quite!" Gavin suddenly disappears from your sight with a flourish of his arms. You gasp, then realize he has used the elven cloak.

Slag lowers you to the ground, but keeps his cold claws firmly wrapped around you. "Where are you, little sting?" the creature asks, looking around.

The treasure heap explodes with coins. "Here!"

Then a stalactite falls from the roof nearby. "And here!" And then Slag cries out as a bright-red scratch appears along his claws. "And here!"

The dragon rears menacingly, then lowers his snout. "I see your point!" You are suddenly free to run, and you bolt as far away from the beast as you can. "A little fun, just a smidgen—tell me who robs me and answer my riddle, and I will set you free."

Gavin appears beside you. "Done!" He points up the blue tunnel. "There is a band of brigands and orcs tunneling and mining around the lake. They know of you—that's how you got your last dinner—and that antechamber there"—he turns and points to another opening—"has a hole they've opened up. When you are sleeping, they sneak in and steal whatever they can reach."

The dragon turns his head and spots the hole. His jaws open in a dragonish smile. "They will receive a shocking surprise next time," he remarks. "Now for my riddle: In the beginning I seem mysterious, but in the end I am nothing serious. What am I?"

You can feel the tension in Gavin's body. The thoughts in your head whirl as you try to think what the dragon refers to. Slag lowers his snout, his huge head coming closer and closer. The silence in the cave grows so thick you can hear the slow drip of water upon the cave floor.

Suddenly you give out a shout! "I have it—the riddle itself!"

Slag drops his snout in disappointment. "Indeed, noisy worm . . . you have it. Well, a bargain is a bargain." At that, the dragon lifts his tail, and you see an opening.

Gavin grabs your arm and you scurry around the dragon, into the tunnel. You run as fast as you can go, afraid the dragon might change his mind. As you bolt upward, fresh air hits your face. Soon, you are free!

Gavin hugs you under the night sky. "You were brave," he says.

"And you!"

"I'm sorry about the caravaners and your father."

A tear stings the corner of your eye. "We did all we could . . . but at least . . ."

He takes your chin and holds your face up so that he may reach it as he bends down. "Yes?"

"I mean . . . that is . . ."

Gavin smiles. "Yes! I have found you!" And he silences any other thought you may have with a warm and unsettling kiss.

END ADVENTURE

PATHWAY 26

"No thanks," you call out. You stand braver than you feel. As you try to walk away, your boots crunch on something littering the cavern floor. Bones!

Ugh! But you feel a little better. With this many meals wandering in over the years, you aren't quite so afraid Slag will eat you.

"Maiden!" calls Slag suddenly.

You look up—right into his amber eyes. Your mind swims! You are trapped by the pull of his powerful thoughts.

"Come closer," he coaxes, and you do, helpless to disobey him. He bends down, his jaws yawning. His fangs are as large as you are as he lowers them about you.

But he very carefully chews the rope from your wrists. As he rears up, he looks down at you in amusement. "Now you must free me."

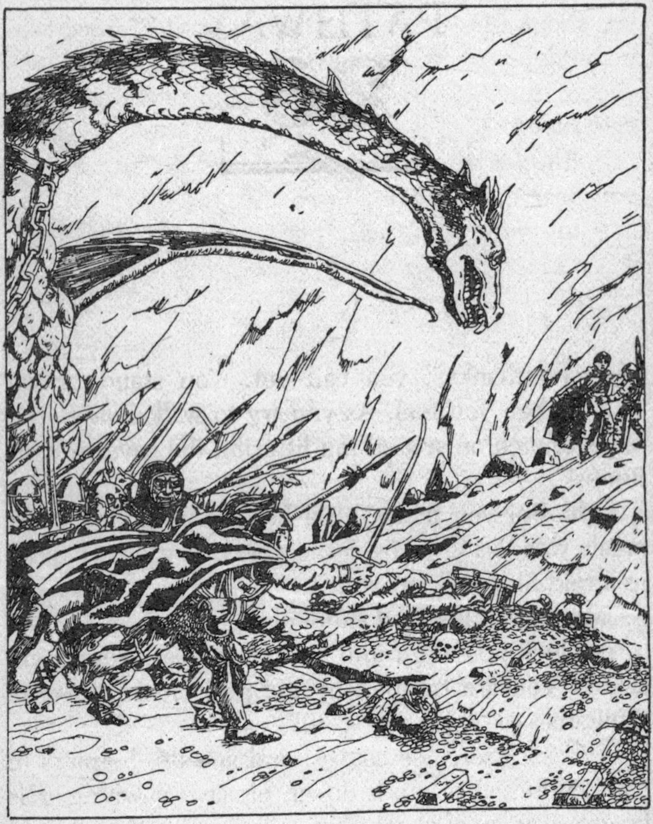

You know you can't. You try to fill your mind with the sensation of being in love with Gavin. You think of his kiss and what he means to you, after all the danger the two of you have been through. "Never!" you shout, but your body is moving toward the chains.

Suddenly, Slag twists away, peering into the shadows of the cavern. "Who goes there? I smell you, new blood. Keep away from us!"

As the fog of your enchantment drifts around you, you hear the answer: "Leave her be, Slag! Let's see you toy with some real power!" Sparks fly from a stalactite as a shining sword wielded by the invisible intruder cuts it down.

Slag hisses and curls his body around, searching for the invader.

Is that Gavin you hear? Or are you dreaming? you wonder. The whole cavern looks like a mist-filled memory. You see orcs gathering at a tunnel entrance, jumping up and down and brandishing spears. Vaguely, you wonder why they have come.

Slag stares down at you. "Little meat! You bring nothing but trouble!" His blue snout wrinkles as he draws his lips back and takes a deep breath.

"Tyrna!" a voice cries by your side. A kiss burns your lips, and the fog disappears! The dragon's spell is broken.

Gavin drops the cloak as he takes your hand. "Run for it!" he shouts and pulls you aside just as a lightning bolt crackles behind you.

You and Gavin race across the cavern. Orcs boil into the chamber behind you, shouting oaths at both the dragon and the Ranger. Slag hisses a dragon curse and hurls himself after you. He has forgotten his chains!

A column shatters. Pieces of it fly like arrows, narrowly missing the two of you. An eerie wailing splits the air as the roof begins to sag. Then it cracks like thunder and blue waters pour into the cavern. Dragon, orcs, and treasure are caught in the flood as Gavin drags you up into a tunnel.

"Keep running," he commands, pulling you after him, as water crashes on your heels. The tunnel leads up and up, and fresh air blows in your faces.

As you break into the open, you see you are at the base of the great wooden gate which dammed the lake. The huddled figures of sleeping caravaners greet you. The two of you awaken them and cut them free, as the gate sways and groans.

All of you scramble free as water gushes from below and pours into the riverbed, to flow across the wasteland.

Gavin smiles as you shout with joy. "Everything is back as it was planned by the gods." He pulls you close to him. "Even as your crossing my path must have been planned. My love for you was surely written in the Book of Fate." He whistles for Stormseeker, and as you wait for the stallion, Gavin holds you tightly.

END ADVENTURE

PATHWAY 27

"All right, Kolroth," Gavin calls. "The answer is yes!" as you put your chin up defiantly.

The cleric smiles widely, wringing his hands in delight. He motions for a guard to blindfold you, but even as you stand in the dark, your sword is pressed into your hand. You resist the temptation to strike out, knowing you are ringed by the enemy.

Kolroth takes you by the hand and leads you. Gavin walks near you, for you can feel his warm and reassuring presence. Soon, you realize your steps are going downward, and the night air is being replaced by musty, stale air. You must be underground! Water drips. You go down, down, down until you are stopped.

The blindfold is ripped from your head, and Kolroth stands smiling. He holds a torch, and the orange light gleams in the cave.

"This is the wellhead of the Ashkaraneth," he says.

You look at the immense pool. You must be in the center of the mountain! The sacred waters are murky and deep. From time to time, an oily ripple disturbs the surface.

Gavin groans. "What have you done?" he asks with dismay.

Kolroth does not answer, only smiles wider. "The bottle is below on the bottom. This stick"—he holds it out—"is magical. It will light once in the water—thus you will be able to see below. There are water beetles about! That's why she has her sword. Yours, I will keep. Stay away from that passage when you return! Only death will meet you down there!" The guards murmur in fear as Kolroth points across the pool. The cleric laughs. "And stay away from the beetles! They are undoubtedly hungry."

Gavin eyes the pool. He leans and whispers, "You'll be all right."

You don't feel certain about it. Your heart pounds in your ears. If only Kolroth had not brought guards with him, you'd attack him right now!

Gavin clasps your free hand. "Jump!" And the two of you plunge into the pool.

The magic stick bursts into a white flare. As you drop into the pool's depths, you hold your breath desperately. You see the potion resting on the bottom, but your lungs feel about to burst. Even as you scoop up the stoppered glass vial, something giant scoots along the sands toward you!

Gavin holds your sword arm down. He hugs you, and points. It is an immense spider. Gavin wants you to follow him and it. Scarcely able to hold your breath another second, you stumble along the sandy bottom after the creature to a nest of rocks and something translucent. Gavin pushes you into a chamber—and you are trapped!

He joins you, saying, "Breathe! These are air bubbles, brought down by the spider for its nest!"

You do so, cautiously. You are inside a huge bubble which quivers and dances around you. The furred and frightening face of the water spider looks in at you. You scuttle into Gavin's arms, ready to scream.

"Don't be frightened! They're friendly. We'll stay down here on the bottom until Kolroth must be sure we've drowned or been eaten. My friend there tells me there are many water beetles around. Move carefully, or the bubble will burst."

He takes the potion from your hand and examines the bottle. "This is deadly! Kolroth can bring cities to their knees with this! He must never have it!"

You brush your loosened hair from your face. You watch as Gavin pushes close to the bubble's wall and appears to be conversing with the water spider. He comes back. "Sit down, Tyrna, and rest awhile." He sits down and draws you into his arms with a comforting embrace.

After a long rest, the water spider returns with several of its kind. You and Gavin take a deep breath and emerge slowly from the bubble chamber. The spiders swim by your side as you surface.

Gavin helps you out. The two of you stand dripping on the tunnel floor. "I'm going to rig up a little surprise for Kolroth if he comes back. I want you to go down that tunnel a ways and wait for me." He points to the passageway leading still farther down the tunnel that Kolroth and his men feared. He takes your sword as he leaves. "I'll catch up as soon as I can. Take the potion with you, just in case."

With misgivings, you make your way down into the tunnel mouth. Gavin disappears into the darkness. As your eyes adjust, you see the dim figure of Kolroth creeping down toward the pool. He will surprise Gavin! You can't let him be hurt! You must either fight with the cleric, though your very bones ache with weariness, or you must warn Gavin and flee down the dank tunnel.

1. *If you struggle with Kolroth, turn to Pathway 57 (page 201).*
2. *If you warn Gavin and the two of you flee down the tunnel, see Pathway 54 (page 191).*

PATHWAY
28

You duck your face away.

"What is it?" Gavin asks with a mysterious smile.

"Nothing! Just . . . be careful, that's all."

He nods, puts on the hooded cloak, and disappears toward the sound of the orcs.

Afraid to be left alone, you inch down the corridor yourself. Soon, you can see by the light of dim lamps a large chamber where the orcs have been mining and damming. Another tunnel stretches toward the surface from the other side. The wooden structure of the watergate extends all the way to the cave floor. From the looks of it, the orcs have been here for months!

Huddled nearby are the caravaners. You see Ranth with his head bowed over the shackles on his wrists. Clearly, they will spend the rest of their lives on the mining project. You must set them free!

To the side lies a pile of treasure, glittering evilly in the twilight. You can see more treasure, jewels and coins and metal objects, buried in the earthen wall on the far side of the chamber. Digging tools are scattered at the wall's base. Many orc hands have been busy digging out the loot. You force your gaze away as the treasure fills your mind with greedy thoughts. You shrink back into the corridor.

Gavin appears suddenly by your side. You jump, startled, but muffle the noise.

"It's done," he tells you. "Now, if it only works."

Soon, the halls ring with the orc cry of "Elves! Elves in the caves!" as they run to and fro. One of them, a horny-skinned nasty-looking creature, bigger and meaner-looking than the others, brandishes the cloak over his head.

"Torg finds elf, Torg kills elf!"

They race in the other direction, spilling toward the surface through the other tunnel. Gavin has laid a false trail, and they follow it with hoarse cries of orcish hatred. You shudder to hear their voices.

You pull your dagger and run quickly to the captives. You still Ranth's cry of fear with a gentle hand. "It's me, Tyrna!"

"Praise the sun!" the caravaner cries, grateful tears in his eyes as you break his shackles open. Gavin works on the others, and soon all are free.

You hesitate. The watergate stretches into the ceiling above you and goes far behind that. There is no way to destroy it from below.

Gavin grabs your arm. "Leave it! I will come back later! This way, and quickly!"

You follow the Ranger's lead through many twisting tunnels, always going upward. After a long, breathless climb, you hear a sound like thunder.

"The falls," Gavin says. He points, and a finger of light stabs into your sight. "The top of the mountain."

He has brought you all the way around the lake and up! The caravaners cheer and pour out into the sunlight. As you reach it, Gavin takes your hand and leads you forth. You blink for a moment.

He holds your hand tightly. "I'm sorry, Tyrna. I couldn't let you follow Torg and kill him to avenge your father."

You shrug. "I've had enough death, anyway. We got the caravaners free—and that's what counts!" You smile mysteriously. "My father would have liked it better this way, anyhow."

You bring something from under your mail shirt and lay it on the ground. The sun strikes it, and the dragon treasure lies glittering. "I managed to save this—for you."

Gavin picks it up with a murmur of appreciation. "It's a magical bridle! Fit for the children of Pegasus—even Stormseeker would be proud!" He laughs. "And I have something for you!" He pulls something out of his belt and holds it out in the palm of his hand.

It's a jeweled comb, beautiful and simple in its curves. "It holds the spells of protection . . . so that even if I am not with you, you will be safe from most evil. But . . . you'll let me be with you, won't you? Come home with me, Tyrna." He embraces you tightly. "Our love is the best thing we've done on this quest of yours . . . but it's more than enough, don't you think?"

END ADVENTURE

PATHWAY 29

Taking your courage, you plunge ahead into the eerie blue light. The tunnel floor dips sharply and you go sliding downward. Gavin catches up and halts you.

"Don't you go without me! Sometimes you put your feet before your brain! I don't want anything happening to you."

"Why on earth would you care?" you say meanly and are instantly sorry. But his reaction to you has you baffled.

"Because I think I love you, that's why!"

"Love me? You haven't even kissed me!"

"I'll take care of that right now," he says and grabs you. He settles the matter with a firm, passionate kiss. You are breathless as he sets you back on your feet. "Now mind!"

You follow him meekly down the passage to the

edge of the immense, blue-colored cavern. A startling sight greets your eyes.

The blue glow comes from the crystal cavern roof above you—the basin that holds the waters of Lake Ashkaraneth! Sunlight filters through, giving everything an eerie look. The roof is supported by immense crystal pillars, beautiful carved columns—and chained between them is a huge blue dragon!

Slag is not dead! You gasp in amazement, even as the tail of the dragon moves in his sleep.

Gavin draws you back inside the passage hurriedly. "A blue dragon breathes lightning bolts, not fire! Always let a sleeping dragon lie."

But the two of you creep cautiously to the cavern mouth, drawn by the wondrous sight. Huge stalactites and stalagmites hang from the ceiling and push their way up from the floor. Crystals shine in the colors of the rainbow. And everywhere lies treasure, all the treasure the rapacious dragon accumulated before his downfall.

Whoever chained Slag devised a clever punishment. Most of his treasure cannot be reached—and one pull too strong or too far on his chains, and the roof will come tumbling down, inundating him. You don't feel sorry for the beast. Slag must have destroyed hundreds of villages, and he turned the land outside into a wasteland. It is a just punishment.

"Now I know why the orcs are mining. The dragon has probably summoned them."

"But how?"

"Evil calls to evil, though silently. They are plundering the treasure. Undoubtedly, Slag has been trying to talk them into unchaining him."

This can never be! "We must kill him, then."

Gavin shakes his head. "He serves the sentence the gods deemed fair. I don't want to meddle with what Neron did. But something must be done!"

Your whispering voices echo throughout the cavern. Suddenly, the dragon rouses. You turn your head away, afraid to look toward his eyes as he peers around trying to find you.

"Mortal meat! Come closer. Slag has much to offer you!" His voice is compelling. It carries a spell.

Gavin grips your hand tightly. "Don't listen to him!"

You moan. "We've got to do something, Gavin. I can't stand it. We've either got to slay him or leave quickly!"

He frowns. "Or perhaps I can find a way past him. I see other tunnels leaving the chamber. That would be dangerous and tricky, though."

As the two of you hesitate, Slag calls out, "Many things have I here! I will reward you handsomely, if you would remove these shackles of mine!"

Suddenly, you find pity for him. You would like to help the blue dragon, though your thoughts scream at you that he is a wicked, wicked beast.

"Hurry," you tell Gavin, as you weaken.

1. If the two of you decide to attempt slaying the dragon, go to Pathway 47 (page 171).

2. If you retreat, see Pathway 32 (pathway 124).

3. Or if, knowing you must find another way out, you decide to slip past the dragon, turn to Pathway 20 (page 80).

PATHWAY
30

Before Gavin can agree, you spit out, "I would rather die first!"

Kolroth's face stretches in his evil smile. "Then you shall," he declares. He signals his followers.

By torchlight, you are marched to the edge of the cliff. The dark sky stretches overhead. The waters of the Ashkaraneth wait far below.

Kolroth makes a few signs over your heads. You shudder as Gavin exclaims, "You're the one poisoning the lake!"

"That, and more! When I am done, the waters of the Ashkaraneth will be boiled down to a mere flaskful—but what a potion within that flask! I can conquer the world!" Spear and sword points dig into your back. "Drive them off!"

"Wait!" The Ranger asks. "A last goodbye." Then Gavin, who has been staring intently into the waters below as they froth up, kisses you briefly on your forehead, but he whispers, "Don't worry," as he does.

"Touching," sneers Kolroth. "Push them over!"

With a sharp stab in your back, you and Gavin take a running leap and are over. The wind whistles past your ears as you fall. Your heart is pounding in fear. Then you crash into the water, and plunge deep below. Your lungs sob for air as you finally bob to the surface. Gavin swims over and hugs you.

"I spotted water spiders—they should help free us," he tells you. "The Ashkaraneth is stronger than Kolroth!"

But even as he speaks, the water ripples as hungry creatures surround you, their mandibles snapping. Water beetles, not water spiders!

Perhaps Gavin was wrong! Now you must swim your fastest to make it to the shore in time to escape!

END ADVENTURE

PATHWAY
31

You stagger to a halt and hang your head down. Gavin stops. You cannot see his face as you say, "I'm sorry. I—I can't keep going. My head thinks it's a drum, and the water skin is nearly empty."

You raise your face, but you don't have the courage to look at him. Heat waves shimmer off the sands, and you think you see dancing waters in the distance.

You finally glance at Gavin and see a smile flicker across his face as he says, "That's all I need to know. A foolish warrior is soon a dead one."

What is it you see in his eyes? He gives a shrill whistle, and a beautiful white stallion comes trotting up from out of nowhere. His silken hide is dappled with clouds of charcoal gray. "This is Stormseeker. At my command, he will carry you."

The intelligent creature whickers and eyes you as you admire him.

Gavin turns. "As for water, the Ashkaraneth is ahead of us. The orcs, it appears, needed water as badly as you, for the trail shows they have already been here and gone." He gives you a leg up onto the horse and walks by your side toward the mirage. But blue waters do not appear. Gavin appears puzzled as he leads Stormseeker forward. They stop, and you believe he must be conversing with the stallion, as a Ranger has the ability to do.

Gavin looks at you, faintly worried. "Stormseeker says that he barely catches the scent of water. I don't understand it. Stay here." And he leaves you in the shelter of a broken rock while he runs forward to the mirage.

The instant he breaks the image of water, a shriek fills the air. Whirling sand blasts the distance between you. It is a sand devil, towering above you, headed right at you! Stormseeker rears.

Gavin yells, "Run! Run while you can!"

The sand devil veers at the sound of his voice. Prey on foot attracts it. The spout of sand and gravel heads toward him. As Stormseeker whinnies and dances in fear, you watch it traveling toward Gavin. Its pattern is a little odd, almost circular. You are almost too frightened to think straight, but you must! You might be able to reach Gavin before it does and carry him out of reach of the vortex. On the other hand, the sand devil seemed to think you more of a menace than Gavin. You might have a chance attacking it directly.

Gavin shields his face from the blasting force of the

whirling monster. You must kick Stormseeker into immediate action—but which?

1. Will you and Stormseeker try to rescue Gavin before the sand devil reaches him? Turn to Pathway 13 (page 54).

2. Or will you risk attacking the mysterious force, not knowing if your sword will even have an effect on it? Turn to Pathway 22 (page 86).

PATHWAY 32

Gavin pulls you away as you cry, "Don't kill him, Gavin!" He picks you up in his strong arms and carries you swiftly from the blue chamber.

As he hurries up the tunnel, dirt and gravel slipping under his boots, he stumbles. The two of you fall against the cave wall—and it gives way, letting you into yet another passage.

Gavin dusts you off. "Are you all right?"

"Yes . . . I think so." You press your hands to your head. "I never want to hear that dragon say another word!"

He looks about. The passageway is dark and you can barely see his form. "Orcs again," he says finally. "They've been digging in here." He takes your hand and leads you. "We've got no choice but to try to find our way out of here."

As you stumble along, he keeps a firm grip on you.

You remember his kiss and feel your face heating up. You must glow in the dark!

Suddenly, Gavin stops and shushes you. The harsh tone of orc voices reach you, three or four arguing, when a loud bass rumble interrupts.

"Nar, Patch! I can smell elf a league away! I tells you . . . one's been here."

"Where? Where? Only Slag up ahead where we hid entrance to blue tunnel. And Slag eats elves, too."

"Eats elves?" you gasp, before Gavin presses your mouth shut with the palm of his hand.

"Torg smells elves! You a coward . . . go on back. I looks for elves."

The second orc squeals, a high-pitched conniving sound. It makes you shudder to hear him. Gavin begins to tug your elven cloak of concealment free from his belt. There is a slap and another squeal.

The danger of fighting orcs in a dark tunnel is clear, yet the cloak will only work for one of you. As the rough-faced leader slaps his mates around and forces them to search for you, you must decide whether to hide or fight the orcs.

1. *If you choose to hide, go to Pathway 38 (page 142).*
2. *See Pathway 56 (page 198) if you decide to fight the orcs.*

PATHWAY 33

"Neron was only one!" you say, as you lower your sword. "He defeated Slag, despite the odds. I can find aid if you'll guide me to the temple."

He turns so that you cannot see his face. "I can't do that. I am the Warden of Ashkaraneth, and there has been trouble at the river. You must cross the river to its source and then go up into the mountains." He adds, "Reason advises against it. The land talks to me. Someone or something is rousing old evil. That is why I came as Warden from the valleys. The river doesn't flow as it should, yet the gods told my people that it would never dry."

"Could it be the orcs?"

"I don't know." Gavin turns to look at you, a faint breeze ruffling his hair. You think that he is handsome in his way and wonder what your father would have thought of him. He wears a Ranger's garb and carries a sword of elven make.

"Take me with you to the river, then I'll go on my own and be out of your way!" You determinedly sheathe your weapon. You will not be left behind. "My father was taking me to the Warrior Games. I can ride, use a sword—I'm even good with a bow."

"You have a long journey to finish."

"I'm not going now. You must understand. I can't just leave him here, without a burial or a tribute or anything! At the temple, maybe I can find another warrior or the gods to help me."

He shakes his head. "You are young and pretty, even for a human girl. The wastes are harsh, Tyrna. I must follow my duty and send you back to my people where you'll be safe until I can guide you past the mountains. I'll come back and get you when I know what disturbs the Ashkaraneth. I will help the caravaners, if I can."

"But that's my job!"

Gavin raises his head and whistles. At his call, a horse appears, trotting from the shrub-covered hills in the distance. He gallops on the horizon, growing magically nearer and nearer, a horse of the purest white dappled with the gray of storm clouds. He is a truly noble animal. You catch your breath at his beauty. He stops in front of you, pawing the ground.

"Stormseeker," Gavin says to him. "I have a human who must be borne back to the valley. Will you carry her for me?"

The large brown eyes of the creature consider you

with intelligence. You think of appealing to it, anything to keep from getting left behind, or your quest will end before it has begun!

If you appeal to Stormseeker, turn to Pathway 6 (page 28).
If you think it is foolish to ask the stallion to help you, see Pathway 15 (page 63).

PATHWAY 34

You stop and remove your light helmet, wiping your brow. You will die before you will admit you can't keep up! Your head throbs in the sun. Gavin eyes you curiously, but he doesn't say anything.

The terrain of the wastes is broken here, very rocky, with small hills that block out the horizon. You perch on a boulder so that you can rebraid your hair, giving you a chance to rest.

Gavin says, "Let me hold that," and takes your helmet for you.

You waste as much time as you can, and when you stand to move off again, your father's cloak falls to the ground. He picks it up. You snatch it from his hands.

"I was only trying to help," the Ranger says.

Embarrassment flames your cheeks. "I—I'm sorry. But it's all I have left now."

"I know. I'm sorry too. But you mustn't think that's all your father gave you, Tyrna. All that you are and much that you will be, you owe to his teaching. Your pride, your grace, your . . ." He stops and looks away.

Suddenly, you sense that he is embarrassed. Was he about to compliment you? "Gavin . . . what were you about to say?"

"Nothing that I have a right to say. I, too, have my parents to thank for what I am—half human and half elf! My father has drilled into me that I must be elven, not human! But you . . . your eyes . . ." He stops, confused.

You draw close to him, looking into his deep violet eyes. You wish you knew how to kiss as his face bends near to yours. You think he is going to. You lean forward, your lips parted slightly, thinking that you must make them soft and gentle—wondering silly things, like where his nose goes and your chin, when suddenly the warmth of his mouth reaches yours.

With a crash and a clang, the peace is broken by the shouts and thumps of orcs! You spring apart as their harsh voices and clamor reach you.

Gavin grabs his sword hilt. "They've doubled back!"

The rocks hide you, but only for the moment. Orcs hate elves with a passion and will attack on sight! Should the two of you stand and fight, or have you a better idea, as you grasp your father's cloak of concealment?

1. Your quest for vengeance can end here. If you fight, see Pathway 43 (page 160).

2. Thinking of a better idea, turn to Pathway 46 (page 168).

PATHWAY
35

Gavin motions for you to put away your bow. He puts his hand on Stormseeker's soft muzzle as the magnificent horse tosses his head nervously. With a gentle word, he begins to lead the stallion down the rocks, out of range of the pack.

You are nearly as nervous as Stormseeker. They are at your back, though still far enough away that they should not be able to see or smell the three of you. Chills run down your spine. You press your knees tightly against Stormseeker's dapple-gray flanks. The stallion tosses his head again and his muscles ripple in fear beneath you.

The terrain is rocky. Gravel rolls from under the stallion's hooves. Suddenly, a flat rock gives way. With a high-pitched squeal, the horse goes down and you are thrown. As your body twists in the air, you remember to go limp. You land heavily, and your head crashes into the dirt—and the world goes dark.

You awaken with fiery stabbing pains all through your body. Your head feels like a drum! Even the cool fingers stroking your forehead don't help much.

Gavin looks down at you anxiously. "Are you all right?"

There are two blond, handsome elven Rangers staring at you. You blink until there is only one. When you try to answer, he places his fingers gently across your lips.

"You're hurt, but not seriously. I can't take you across the desert like this, Tyrna, and you have brought feelings to me that I don't understand. I can't risk your safety. Stormseeker is favoring a leg. He may be lamed. Both of you must come home to my green valleys to heal."

You realize his arms are tightly around you—and it is the best feeling you've had for days. "The caravaners—"

"I promise that I'll send someone after them. Your quest will be fulfilled. I'll even come back myself if you're feeling better. But I don't want to leave you alone until then." He twists around, as the faint sound of the wild dog pack fades away entirely. "Can you stand?"

"Yes . . . I think so."

"Good. It's a long walk home, but you can lean on me all the way." Gavin helps you to your feet. He holds you tightly for a long moment.

Is it your imagination, or do you see things in his eyes that you never saw in a man's eyes before?

Could it be the beginnings of love? You aren't sure, but you know that you suddenly have all the time in the world to find out, as the three of you begin a brand-new journey.

END ADVENTURE

PATHWAY 36

"**M**y father never taught me to be a coward," you say tightly and grip your sword at ready as you start to the front door.

Gavin smiles ruefully as he joins you. As you walk between the darkened columns guarding the empty walkway, your footsteps echo in the abandoned building. Half the dome roof has cracked and fallen away. The temple reminds you of an eggshell broken open.

He touches your arm. "I sense something—" Shouts interrupt him. You freeze in your place as magically lit torches flare up and you find yourself ringed by humans and orcs alike. They leap from behind the columns and you and Gavin are trapped!

Gavin throws his arms up, momentarily blinded by the torchlight. Your swords are knocked to the floor, where they clatter uselessly.

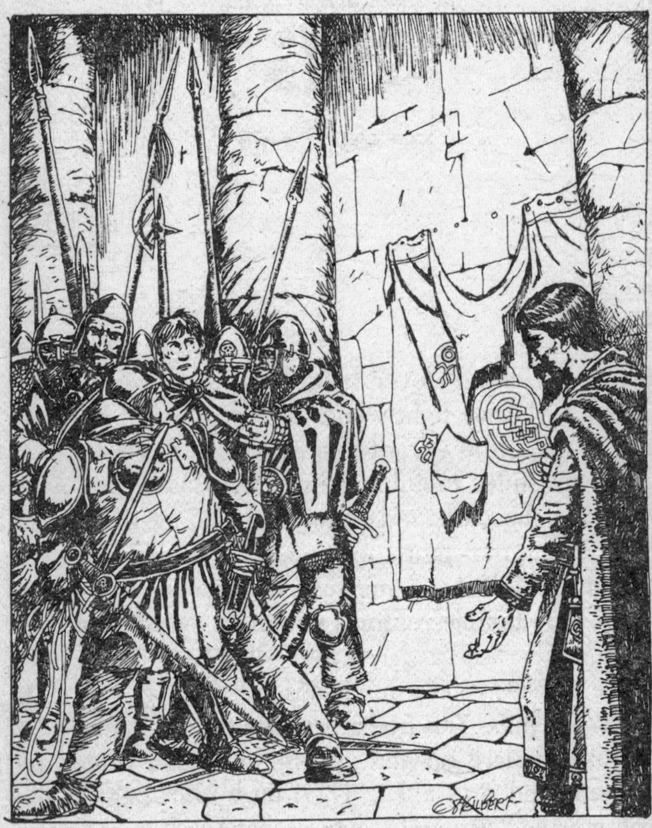

The torn tapestry behind the simple altar parts, and a man strolls out. His black hair is slicked down and his beard oiled to a point. His robes of goodness have been horribly corrupted with the signs of black magic. You swallow your fear and try not to look at him. This explains the reek of evil about Neron's monument!

The cleric waves at his men to stand back after they have pulled your arms behind you and crudely bound your wrists. "I, Kolroth, have foretold correctly! Once again, sacrifices have been delivered to us. We will increase our power tonight! This temple will become mine, utterly and completely, and then the world!"

Shivers run down your back at his crazed words. The poor caravaners! They must have been taken to use as sacrifices!

"We may be more use to you alive than dead," Gavin says quietly. As he stands next to you, you see his hands working gently but firmly at his bonds, testing them.

Kolroth smiles. "Come with me, prisoners. You have information about the outside world I'd like to hear." He beckons you through the tapestry. "Keep watch!" he orders his men before following after you.

You whisper to Gavin, "We can't help this man! He's evil—and crazy!" But Gavin hushes you.

Once inside the secret room that must be Kolroth's chamber—it has a sleeping divan in one corner and is littered with books and scrolls—the cleric faces you triumphantly. He folds his spindly hands together.

His nails glitter in the torchlight, long and pointed like the claws of an animal.

"You wish your freedom?"

"Of course."

"It might be arranged. I would have to fool my worshipers, but it would be worth it. There is a certain bottle, contents unimportant to you, that lies at the bottom of the wellhead from which springs the Ashkaraneth. Fetch it for me!"

You strain to be free, saying, "No, Gavin, we can't do this!"

Without looking at you, Gavin says, "I'd rather be alive than dead. Leave us, Kolroth, while I convince her."

With a menacing smile, the cleric leaves the room. Gavin looks at you. "Trust me in this, Tyrna. He'll kill us anyway—but I know his tricks. We'll have a chance to escape if we do the task."

"Or die anyway, having done something horrible for our last deed!" You stand, uncertain. You must decide whether to do the task or refuse it.

1. See Pathway 30 (page 119) if you refuse the task.
2. If you trust Gavin and agree to do what Kolroth wishes, see Pathway 27 (page 107).

PATHWAY 37

"**G**avin!" you shout, pulling at your sword. Torg jumps back, astonished, as you lunge at him.

The Ranger jumps out from the rocks with a clear elven cry. The orcs make a horrible noise as they see him. Gavin laughs. He leaps and climbs away after slashing two of them down. You see a shimmer over his head and he disappears. He is using the enchanted cloak to confuse them.

Torg and Patch shout orders, as the orcs run back and forth in their lust to catch the elven warrior. You stand forgotten. You gasp and can barely stand to watch as their swords thrust and hack at thin air, as Gavin appears and disappears. Orcs run into each other shouting terrible oaths.

Torg slashes the air where Gavin just disappeared again. He cuffs Patch, yelling, "Find him! Kill elf, Patch!"

The orc rolls to the ground, as Gavin's laughter fills the air. Soon, the orcs are racing around in mass confusion, spotting Gavin by the sheen of his sword just before he appears again.

Torg points. "There he goes! After him, after him!" Finally, they rush off into the desert, following what they swear is the invisible elf.

You drop your sword point to the sand. "I hope he makes it," you say softly, thinking of his bravery and your interrupted kiss. "Oh, please be careful and come back for me!"

"Done!" the Ranger says joyfully. The cloak drops to his feet as he appears beside you. You don't even have time to blush as he grabs you. "My heart is stronger than my mind, Tyrna! You're as brave as you are beautiful—and stubborn! I've waited a long time for someone like you. Come home with me, now, or let me go with you on your quest, to keep you safe. Please."

He whistles, and after a long moment, a beautiful dapple-gray stallion trots over the horizon. "This is Stormseeker," Gavin tells you. "He comes whenever I call, no matter how far the distance. He will carry you home for me, or wherever I command him."

You are filled with awe as you look at him. You realize he is a true elven horse. Other wonders might await you in the valleys of Gavin's home.

Gavin adds, "The lake is not far from here. The caravaners may be hidden in the caves and tunnels that the dragon Slag used. I can take you into them by a back way, through the falls that empty into the lake. It'll be dangerous, Tyrna. The orcs will come back! It's up to you."

As you look into his eyes, you remember that your father used to lecture you for not knowing when you were beaten. He would want you safe. Going home sounds like a good idea, but your obligation to his memory is important to you, too. You must consider very carefully what you will do now.

1. *Go to Pathway 16 (page 66), if you wish to go home with Gavin.*

2. *If you wish to pursue your quest, turn to Pathway 7 (page 33).*

PATHWAY
38

You push the cloak into Gavin's hands firmly. "You take it!" And before he can argue, you run and conceal yourself in a crevice in the earthen tunnel. Gavin ducks down and disappears beneath the cloak as the gang of orcs enters the passageway.

They are still arguing. You can see the leader, a big brute with a scar running down the length of his face. He gnashes his teeth. The other orcs look around, sniffing and making horrible noises.

"Smell there! Torg smells elf, all right!" He swings his club threateningly.

A smaller, narrow-faced orc whines, "Torg big, brave leader!"

But Torg isn't pleased and bats him aside as he strides past your hiding place. "Shaddup, Patch!"

Patch falls back—right at your feet. You freeze, hoping the shadows hide you, but he looks up and your eyes meet. You realize that orcs have pretty good eyesight in the darkness. There is no doubt he has seen you when he begins to shout.

"Elf! Elf warrior! Elf! Torg!" But he is too scared, thank goodness, to swing his weapon at you.

Torg lumbers back and pulls you out of the shadows. He looks you up and down, his tusks showing and his nostrils sniffing. "Not elf. Human." He growls in disappointment, then smiles. The nasty grimace makes you shiver. "Slaves dig a new tunnel—right under Slag's jaws. Lots of nice treasures there—but Torg afraid Slag is hungry. Let's feed this one to Slag. Make it easier to get treasure!"

The orcs bound up and down in eager agreement. As you stand in dismay, they tie your wrists and push you roughly before them. You leave Gavin hidden behind as they march you toward their destination.

They argue as they march you along. You gather they want to slay the blue dragon, but are afraid of it. Just as you hope they will be so busy batting each other around they'll forget you, the new tunnel opens up with a brilliant blue glow. You are headed for Slag again! Your heart sinks with fear.

Torg shoves you in the back. "Get in there, dragon meat!" And you fall into the cavern!

You roll into the cavern and look up—practically under the dragon's snout. You stifle a scream as the beast looks down at you. It's only a matter of time before it blasts you. You tell yourself to be calm. If you can get to the other side of the cavern, to where you were when you and Gavin first spotted the dragon, you might be able to get free.

Your helmet rolls loose at your feet, no longer any protection. Your hair lies free over your shoulders.

"Ahhh," sighs the blue dragon. "Back so soon? Forgotten me, I thought you had. Come closer, little bite."

His honeyed voice begins to charm you again. You try not to listen to it. You accidentally look into his eyes. They are like huge, amber jewels. You force your gaze away.

Surely Gavin has followed you and will be here to help. The orcs have scurried away, afraid Slag may try to blast them. They won't be back until they're sure you've been eaten.

"You're a pretty thing," Slag says. "You remind me of the maidens they used to throw me for dinner. But I won't eat you for dinner. Come closer."

In spite of yourself, you do. You struggle to free your hands as you kick through the dragon treasure.

"Ahhhh," sighs the beast again. "You are a maiden! What things I could give you. Kingdoms of your own. Jewels. Crowns. Men begging to pay court to you—and, at night, you could fly on dragon wings. Let me chew those bonds away from your hands."

How does he know what you wanted? Can he read your mind? All the things you hoped to earn at the Warrior Games and more does the wily creature begin to offer you. Your head feels thick and heavy, as though you can barely hold it up. Suddenly, it doesn't seem important to wait for Gavin. You are powerful, and with a blue dragon as your friend, you can rule the world on your own.

Slag bends his face very close to yours. His blue

scales shine in the light that glows down from the crystal ceiling. "I promise to be your slave, maiden, only free me. Unloose my chains! I will do anything you want."

You can control Slag! He will find the orcs that killed your father and avenge you, and then he will take you away from here, to whatever glorious adventures the two of you can find!

Will you take what the dragon offers you or will you wait for Gavin to rescue you?

1. *If you wish to use the dragon's power to avenge your father, see Pathway 53 (page 189).*

2. *Go to Pathway 26 (page 103), if you wish to wait for Gavin to save you.*

PATHWAY
39

"Just remember, it's your idea," you say to Gavin.
The two of you back away from the chamber hastily. No one follows, and the mumbling stops. You check your helmet to make sure your braids are still tucked up inside.

He throws the hooded cloak on and follows. The two of you stagger into the larger tunnel, singing in what you hope are drunken voices. Orcs and brigands roll at your feet. You leap to avoid them.

Gavin growls and shoves you aside. You shove back, and step by step, you gain the direction of the chamber where the caravaners are supposed to be stowed. Torchlight flickers as an opening ahead goes downward, bringing a strange scent with it. Also, the golden air now has an eerie blue tinge to it. Just as you are about to remark on the strangeness to Gavin, a fighter enters the cavern, waving a jug. He stands head and shoulders above the rest. You stop as you spot the crooked crown. Seen easily in the torchlight, you can tell he is a tall, handsome brute of a man, with dark curly hair and a short curly beard. His eyes are a piercing blue. The brawl hesitates at the approach of the renegade leader, Loric.

"Oh, oh," Gavin says. "I've got to get you out of here, quickly! Pretend to drop!"

Before you can say a startled yes, he swings at you with a curse. The blow lands on the side of your helmet and you fall over, right on cue.

Gavin leans down and slings your limp body across his shoulders. "Owe me money, does you?" he growls and begins to stagger off, carrying you. No one pays any attention as you draw near Loric.

But you are hanging upside down. Your helmet falls suddenly, and your long red braids tumble out. Gavin freezes in his tracks.

"Hey! What's this?" Loric straightens, lowering his jug of ale. "What have you there, mate? A girl, by the looks of it!"

Gavin turns as the fighter blocks his path.

"Put her down, by gar!"

"She's mine!" Gavin retorts as he sets you on your feet.

Loric reaches out and fondles one of your braids. "Never ceases to amaze me," he says, "How did you smuggle her in, eh? Well, the jig's up. I want her." He takes your chin in his hand and turns your face from side to side. "A beauty, too, under all that dirt. I been needin' a queen."

"Dirt!" you say. Then, in astonishment, "Queen?"

"That's right! Get me enough gold, I'm going to sweep across the desert and conquer the world. Make myself king! You ever want to be a queen, huh?" His dirty fingers trail across your cheek.

You shrink back. Gavin takes your arm. "She stays with me!"

Loric grabs the other arm and begins to pull you away. "I'm your leader, and I takes what I wants! Do as I say, or it's the blue tunnel for you, just I did with them pesky, complaining caravaners!"

Orcs and fighters alike gasp and stop their brawling.

You are stretched between them. Gavin can't do much without revealing his elven identity, for which they will kill him instantly, if they can. On the other hand, the blue tunnel seems to be feared. The two of you can escape down it, possibly without anyone even bothering you.

"Gavin!" you protest. "Do something! I feel like a wishbone!"

Gavin gives you an odd smile. "It's your choice," he answers. "Do you want to be a queen or come with me?"

Loric pulls harder. "You got no choice, girl! Your boyfriend will be sorry the minute I stuff him in the tunnel. No one ever comes back from there alive! Besides, I want you for my bride," he adds with a drunken sneer.

Being a queen sounds pretty good compared to being dead! You might be better off to distract Loric and hope Gavin can rescue you later, without all the orcs and brigands around. On the other hand, Loric scares you. Will you ask Gavin to reveal himself and save you, carrying you off into the blue tunnel, or will you let Loric take you away?

1. Turn to Pathway 10 (page 44) if you will let Loric take you for his bride.
2. If you call for Gavin's help and risk the blue tunnel, see Pathway 25 (page 97).

PATHWAY
40

"Be careful," you tell him softly.

You lean forward hesitantly, not quite sure how your lips should be. But when they touch his, your mouth melts and the warmth of his floods you. The moment sends tingles all through you as he kisses you back. You think that your father was right to worry you might choose being in love over becoming a warrior! But as you back away, opening your eyes, you see Gavin frowning at you.

"Now is not the time," he says sternly. 'You human girls!"

"You're part human, too!" you answer. You are stung by his elvishness. He relents and touches your face gently.

"There will be time enough for all things later," he adds, but you turn away, totally embarrassed already.

He slips away with your cloak, leaving you to wait

behind. You can see a little in the grayness. You spot a cleft in the tunnel wall and wedge your slender body into it, crouching in the shadow. The blush of your embarrassment makes your face feel red-hot, and you keep pressing your cold hands to your cheeks to cool them. What feels like long afterward, the tunnel begins to echo with the tramp of boots.

Gavin comes down the tunnel swiftly, the elven cloak in one hand and another cloak in the other. You hiss at him.

"Over here!"

He joins you in the hiding place, spreading the elven cloak over both of you.

"What's wrong?"

"Too many!" Gavin says anxiously. "I stole another cloak for disguise, but I couldn't find the caravaners."

The two of you huddle under the cloak as the tunnel fills suddenly with both human brigands and orcs. They are weaving and carrying jugs of wine and ale about with them, quarreling about their leaders. The names Loric and Torg are shouted.

"Narr . . . if Torg's such a great leader of orcs, why does our Loric have to tell him what to do!" says one mean-faced ruffian, as he swills his ale.

The orc facing him shows his tusklike teeth in a grimace. "Ain't nobody tells an orc how to mine!"

"Oh, yeah? You couldn't find your two ugly feet if I was to pound your head between 'em!" snarls the fighter. "If you was so great, how come you guys had to go raidin' and bring back the prisoners we got stuffed in the antechamber, now, eh?"

151

Gavin stiffens. He nods at you. The brigand must mean the caravaners! Now you know where they are.

The orc snarls back, "Patience, dogface. Carpen wasn't looted in a day, y'know."

Gavin puts his hands to his mouth and imitates the brigand's voice. "Narr . . . you orcs had to find it first!"

The orc's ugly face twists into a horrible grimace and he swings his fist at the nearest human, and before long, orcs and men are fighting all over the tunnel.

"The caravaners are beyond," Gavin says. "We can get through—or we can go back out. You're taking the biggest risk. I've got the cloak here, and they won't know I'm an elf. They might think you're a brigand, if we cuff each other around. Want to try it?"

Ale jugs crash and bodies thud as the drunken fighters swing at each other—missing more often than not. You gulp. If either of you is discovered, you are in terrible danger, but on the other hand, you know where the caravaners are. How can you quit when you're so close?

1. Go to Pathway 39 (page 146) if you decide to make your way through the brawlers.

2. If you think it wiser to flee, see Pathway 17 (page 69).

PATHWAY 41

The tunnel's glow surrounds you the moment you step into it. You touch your arms as your skin glows eerily. You can see quite well, but the haze gives you the creeps.

Gavin catches up with you. He takes you by the elbow and whispers, "I can see well . . . can you?"

"Yes," you answer in surprise.

You walk forward cautiously. Crystals poke from the tunnel walls, their sharp beauty catching and reflecting the blue light. Your footsteps are muffled. A sound reaches you. It is a loud blowing noise and stops and starts, like a blacksmith's bellows. Gavin pulls you gently behind him and shields you as he takes the lead.

The tunnel grows larger and wider, until you are nearly lost in it.

"There must be a gigantic cavern ahead," Gavin whispers.

The blue light comes from it. You shiver at its strangeness. Gavin pulls you forward cautiously.

"Can you sense anything?" you ask quietly, remembering the elven knowledge of orcs in the other tunnel.

He pauses. "A strange smell, unlike any I've smelled before, and the glow, of course. Do you want to go back or explore the cavern with me?"

Even as he asks, the bellows noise gets louder!

"We came for orcs," you say nervously.

1. Will you explore the cavern? See Pathway 29 (page 115).

2. If you turn back and take the other tunnel, turn to Pathway 9 (page 42).

PATHWAY
42

"I don't like it," you answer. You point with sword tip to the back door. Gavin nods and leads the way.

A heavy tapestry hangs across the wide opening, a weaving of monsters, maidens, and warriors. Once a magnificent piece, it is now old and moldy. You part it gingerly with your sword blade. A solid wall faces you. Gavin runs his hands over it.

"My elven senses should be of some help," he explains. He runs the palms of his hands over a panel and, with a nod of triumph, depresses it. A door clicks open. He pushes it ajar so that you may see in.

Ranth and the others sit huddled in the center of the temple. They are dirty and weary. A cleric is pacing the floor in front of them, his wooden staff striking with every step like a menacing blow. Symbols of black power outline his once holy robes.

He strokes a pointed and oily beard with his free hand.

"Tell me what you know! I will give you no more chances! Armies are gathering—I need to know from where and when they will strike!"

Gavin touches your shoulder. "He fears what he himself is most likely getting ready to do."

"Raise an army?"

"He has the crazed eyes of a true fanatic. He probably believes he has some chosen destiny." Gavin moves around you cautiously. "But where are his followers?"

Before you can venture a guess, the very ground trembles beneath you. You have been kneeling at the doorway to listen, and it knocks you to the ground. Gavin grasps you instantly.

The caravaners cry in fear. With a shout, the cleric quiets them. He raises his arms, his robes falling back. His skin is tattooed, so illustrated with inks and dyes that it appears monsters coil about him! "I, Kolroth, will tame the earth powers! You will be thrown to the Ashkaraneth in sacrifice soon enough, but first tell me what I want to know!"

Ranth spits at him defiantly. Gavin says, "That's just the break I need," as the evil cleric bends over the caravaner, his arm raised to punish.

With a movement like that of a shadow, Gavin is at his back, sword point to his rib, as he takes Kolroth by surprise.

You enter quickly and cut the caravaners free. They stagger up and flee the building, shouting. "Run! Run! The mountain is coming down!"

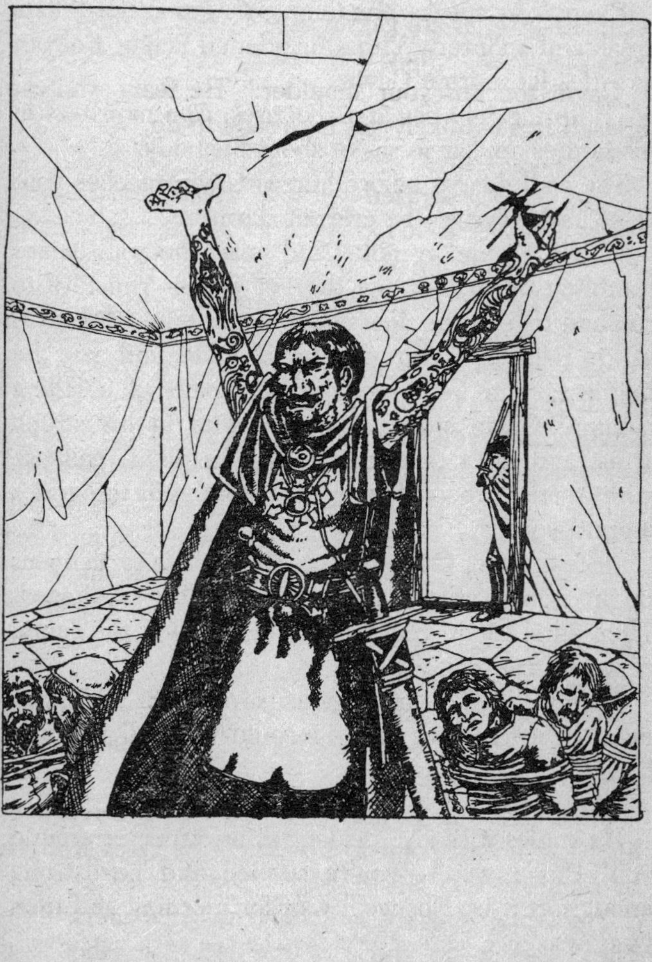

Ranth pulls at your shirt. "Kolroth has dammed the wellhead. The gods are angry! You must leave, and quickly!"

Even as he speaks, the temple shakes again. Pillars creak and splinter. With a maddened laugh, Kolroth wrestles loose from Gavin.

"Help me, my powers!" he cries. The monsters in his tattoos appear to snake about his body.

The wall dances before him as Gavin reaches you. "Get back, Tyrna!" he cries in alarm.

As the ground rumbles and jolts, the wall comes tumbling down, burying the evil cleric. You turn to run and trip on the floor as it buckles beneath you. A sharp pain goes through your ankle and you lie helpless. You lie directly in the path of a falling column! Gavin stoops, picks you up in his strong arms, and races through the exit, as pillars collapse with terrible booms and the temple disintegrates around you.

Once outside, Gavin turns to watch. The earth opens up in gaping cracks, and the temple is swallowed. Then all is silent. Suddenly, you can hear the sound of water, running water.

"The wellhead is free again," says Gavin. He tightens his arms about you. "I could walk all the way home like this."

"You could?"

He smiles with joy. "As long as my arms are around you! But I won't—you're spoiled and headstrong enough as it is. No, we'll wait for morning and then go down."

"Headstrong?" you sputter. "Spoiled?"

"Yes! But not near as spoiled as you're going to be! I shall give you everything, and more!"

Muffled in his embrace, you have but one last thing to say: "All right, only don't put me down right away. I kind of like this."

And he doesn't.

END ADVENTURE

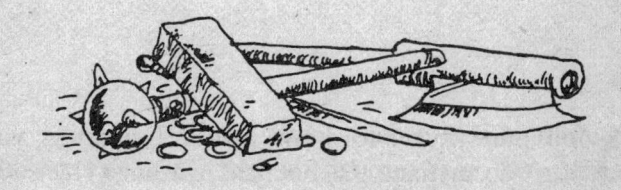

PATHWAY 43

You pull your sword. As Sword Daughter, you can't do anything else but fight to avenge Hamroth. The weapons sing as both you and Gavin draw them together.

Gavin flashes a cold elven smile. "First blood!"

Now you are in your element. You may not know how to kiss, but you can fight. The orcs gnash their teeth as they spill over the rocks toward you. As you back toward a high point, you can see the colorful robes of the caravaners, miserable huddles on the sand below.

The battle is a hard one. You swing your sword until your arms can barely move, the screams of dying orcs filling your ears. Your head is numb and you can scarcely think. Suddenly, you are facing their leader.

He snarls. "I Torg! No one ever kill me!"

Gavin yells, "I'll be there, Tyrna!"

You take a deep breath, knowing this is the one that killed your father. "No! He's mine!" You sweep your helmet from your head.

Torg's jaw drops open in astonishment as your braids fall free. "You girl!" he stammers.

You lower your sword and swing with all your might. As it cuts through his last yell, the remaining orcs run for their lives.

As the orc leader topples, you drop your weapon and stagger away, sick to your stomach. Vengeance is not the sweetness you thought it would be. Your hands are shaking, and you think you might even throw up.

Gavin pats you on the shoulders awkwardly. He says, "Let's cut the prisoners loose."

Legs wobbly, you follow him down. Ranth is grateful, but the others are too battered and exhausted to say anything.

Gavin faces you. You don't know what to say to him. "I—thank you for the kiss. It—it was my first."

He looks away, saying, "The caravaners will take you on your way now."

"Gavin!"

"It was nothing," he adds. "You do not have to thank me."

"I wasn't . . . exactly." Tears sting your eyes. It was nothing to him! "Cold elf!" you cry and turn away.

Gavin shakes his head sadly. "Tyrna, you're a human girl, well taught by your father to be who you are. I carry the same burden from my father. There can be . . . no other way."

You clear your throat and straighten. He is right. You have fulfilled your vow of vengeance. Your first pangs of love will not have a chance to grow here.

Ranth takes your hand in gratitude as he brings you your sword. "We are yours, lady."

"Good," you say, as you sheathe your weapon. "Farewell, Gavin. Perhaps I will see you again someday, at the Warrior Games." You fall into step as you return to the journey you began weeks ago, but this time dreaming of finding love instead of fighting.

END ADVENTURE

PATHWAY 44

You turn and sprint through the shrubbery. Orcs call in confusion behind you.

"What's that?" one growls.

"Rabbit," another mutters.

Despite yourself, you smile. Some rabbit! They crash along behind you, as you desperately dodge through the rocks and brush, looking for a hiding place.

"Oof!" Gavin cries, as you crash into him. He catches you up in his arms. "What's wrong?"

You are so happy to see him! You hug him in relief, and with a raised eyebrow, he hugs you back.

"What's wrong?"

"Orcs! On my trail!"

He pulls you aside. "Down here!" The two of you slide into the earth, orcs hot on your heels. The soft dirt mounds around you, and you plop into a newly dug tunnel. As you race forward, the tunnel stops abruptly at a cave-in. A narrow cleft is all that is left of an opening. Beyond it is unknown.

As you turn, the tunnel to your backs is lit an eerie blue color. Orcs are dropping down from the roof. You must decide quickly whether to squeeze through the cave-in or go back and fight the orcs.

1. *See Pathway 56 (page 198) if you decide to fight the orcs.*

2. *Turn to Pathway 17 (page 69) if the two of you squeeze through the cave-in.*

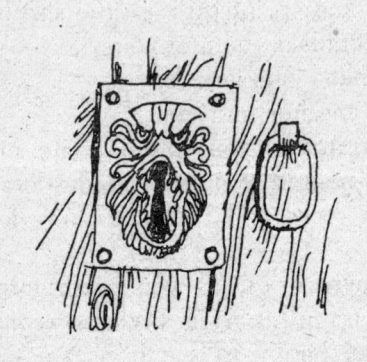

PATHWAY
45

You slide off Stormseeker's back. "The caravaners can't last much longer."

Gavin takes a rope from his pack, saying to Stormseeker. "Wait here for us, but only as long as you're safe."

As you look questioningly at the Ranger, he adds, "There are many creatures that roam the wastes—evil as well as wild. There's even been rumor of a stone troll in the mountains. I can't ask Stormseeker to wait for us if it's not safe."

As he answers you, the stallion tosses his head and trots off to the lake.

You turn your attention to the mountain. It is broken and looks to be a long but easy climb. There are many foot- and handholds from previous climbers. With a deep breath, and reminding yourself that the temple is on the top, you start.

The rock is harsh and cutting. As you get higher and higher, your fingers grow raw. You stop with a cry, and rest on a ledge. Gavin draws even with you.

"What's wrong?"

You hide your hands in your lap, though they hurt terribly. "Nothing."

He reaches out and takes your hands gently. "You're hurt," he says, then kisses each bleeding palm before he bandages you.

You are filled with emotions new to you. Your hands tremble as you loosen them from Gavin's. He smiles, as though reading your thoughts.

The two of you continue climbing as the mountain becomes steeper. Soon, you must use your hand daggers as spikes to pull yourself up. You are near the top. It becomes plain that it has been many years since any pilgrims have come this way to visit Neron's temple.

You pause for breath. "Is it in ruins?" you ask Gavin.

"Is what? Oh, you mean the temple." He shrugs. Wind blows across his face, and you see the dizzying drop to the ground below behind him. "At one time, hundreds used to visit, both this way and on the road. But it's been a long time."

Long to an elf—or even a half-elf—is even longer to you. You shudder, hoping that your trip will not be in vain.

Suddenly, rocks and gravel rain from above. You look up to the shadows, but you can't see anything. You wince and protect your face as more gravel falls.

A strange "uhhhhh" echoes from above. You catch

a glimpse of a long-armed monster grinning down at you, hands dangling.

Gavin grabs you and you freeze to the mountainside. "It's a troll," he whispers in alarm. "There's still some daylight—we might be able to fight it—the temple's just above. Or we can try to get around, or we can go back down."

A troll! They're nearly impossible to defeat! You shudder. Whatever you do, you must do it quickly. The moaning grows louder and stones topple from above you. As the two of you cling precariously to the mountain, you must decide whether to fight the dread monster, flee it, or retreat.

1. If you fight the stone troll, see Pathway 18 (page 72).

2. Turn to Pathway 8 (page 39) if you flee it by trying to climb around.

3. Or, if you retreat back down the mountain, go to Pathway 24 (page 93).

PATHWAY 46

"**S**top! I have an idea!" you cry, and hold Gavin's hand from his sword.

"What are you doing?" he sputters as you throw the elven cloak over his head and push him back into the rocks.

"Hiding you so that the orcs won't find you . . . they'll kill you on sight!" you whisper as you squeeze your own slender body into a ditch beneath a huge boulder. "Now, lie still!"

The orcs clamber over, growling and spitting among themselves. You hear a deep bass voice rumble, "Now we's got a chance to break that treasure free! Them slaves ought to work nicely. Yesss, nicely. Torg has a good idea."

"Sure did, Torg," other orcish voices agree.

Treasure? What treasure? you wonder, as you press farther in under the rock. It sounds as though they are standing right above you.

"Slag left a lot of boo-ti-ful things," the deep-voiced orc says. "Torg has many plans. We dam the river, slaves dig! We all be rich soon. Loric will reward Torg."

"Torg kill Loric," suggested a sly voice. You hear a grunt as one slaps the other.

"Loric a great human leader! Fights wars! Finds us Slag's End with all treasure! You and me play our cards right, we be his guards! Good deal for orcs! Now, shaddup!"

"But Torg! He's taking most of the treasure!" the sly voice protested.

Dust curls about you as another blow lands. The rock shakes and a startled orc thumps to the ground right under your nose. You stare at each other a moment before the nasty creature snarls and grabs your shoulder, dragging you out from under the rock.

"Torg missed a slave! Patch finds it!"

You kick him in the knee, and he drops you. But the other orcs jump forward to ring you, dangerously close to where you have hidden Gavin. If you draw your sword to fight, you will be forcing Gavin out in the open—and orcs surround his hiding place. But if you go with them quietly, Gavin can trail you—and you will be able to find the caravaners, too. You must decide whether to fight or be taken captive as Patch snarls.

"This one has teeth and claws, Torg! Looks more like Loric than others! Maybe we should kill."

You face the hulking leader of the orcs, a nasty-faced big brute with a scar that runs from under the helm of his helmet across his eye to his chin.

1. If you decide to fight to save your skin, see Pathway 37 (page 139).

2. Turn to Pathway 19 (page 75), if you think going quietly is the best thing to do.

PATHWAY
47

"We've no choice," says Gavin grimly, as he pulls his sword.

Slag draws his chains taut, and the crystal columns groan. He searches madly for you, calling. He will pull the roof down in his frenzy!

"Watch him, Tyrna. His breath will blast you, but he can only do it a few times. Then all we must fight are his claws and fangs." Gavin tells you as the two of you separate.

Slag rears high in the cavern, his brilliant blue wings spreading. "Come close, small beings! I shall sear you, then crunch your bones!" His head snakes back and forth as he follows your movements through his glittering treasure.

You suddenly slip on a pile of gold coins. Slag crows in triumph as his claws grasp you. You scream in fear as the dragon hoists you into the air. No

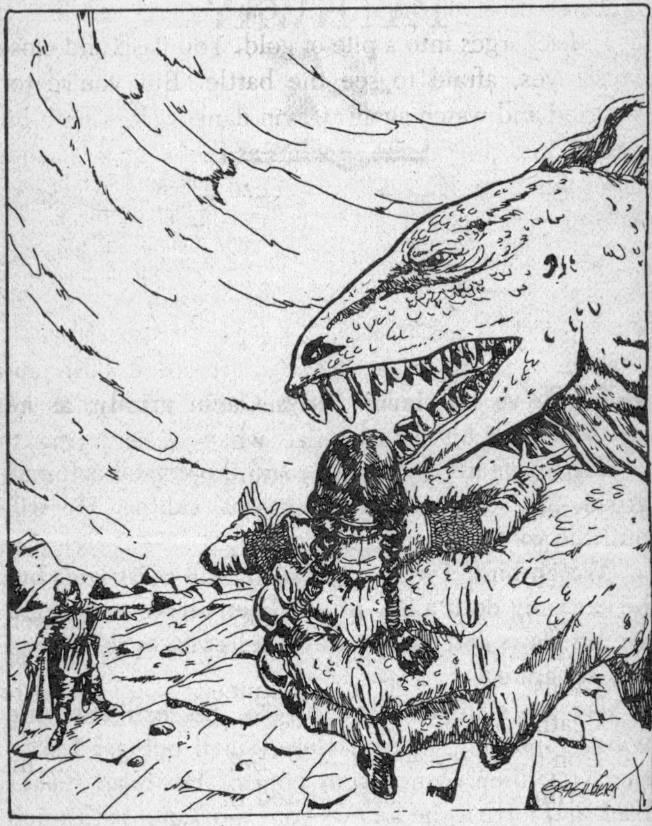

matter how you struggle, his wicked claws are tight around your body.

Gavin charges with an angry yell as Slag turns to him. The dragon's jaws open, and blue lightning crackles through the cavern. Gavin barely dodges it as it discharges into a pile of gold. You gasp and close your eyes, afraid to see the battle. But you're too worried and watch again. Gavin dances close with his sword, and the dragon screams as the weapon slashes along his flank. His claws squeeze tighter about you. You fight for breath.

Gavin leaps across the cavern behind a pillar. As Slag snarls, "Come out, worm!" the elven Ranger charges.

Lightning splits the air with its blue flash and narrowly misses Gavin. But his face looks up at you in triumph, and you realize what he is trying to do—get Slag to use all of his energy, so that his most powerful weapon will be useless!

The Ranger disappears in the shadows. You squirm to look for him. Chains rattle as Slag drops to the ground, hissing. The blue waters above shimmer. The wickedly sharp talons press about you as Slag threatens, "Come out, or I'll squeeze your friend to his death!"

"Don't!" you yell to Gavin, but he walks out, his face grim and his sword pointed in front of him.

"Let her go, Slag," he warns.

Dragon laughter fills the cavern as Gavin charges. Slag rears with a hiss and looses yet another lightning bolt. The ground explodes in front of Gavin. He falls back, knocked down and stunned as the dragon roars in triumph.

"Watch out!" you scream as Slag's clawed foot reaches out, but Gavin rolls away, his shirt tearing. He cleaves with the sword and it is the dragon's turn to scream in pain as one clawed toe is chopped off.

The dragon's jaws open and he breathes again— but no lightning comes out! His breath weapon is used up until he can recharge! Gavin yells in excitement at the knowledge. His sword shining, he dances close. As you watch fearfully, he and the dragon weave in a dance of death. The dragon cries again and again as his claws and fangs snatch at Gavin but miss, and the silver sword strikes again.

Slag suddenly turns his attention to you, his fangs gleaming close. The spiteful dragon intends to swallow you! He brings you to his jaws, and you feel your body begin to slide from his grip into his cavernous mouth!

"Gavin!" you scream in terror.

The Ranger takes a running leap, his sword held with both hands. As he crashes into the dragon's body, he drives the weapon deep into Slag's throat! With a hiss and a thrash, the blue dragon topples. You are breathless as you are thrown to the ground. Slag's tail lashes one last time and the dragon dies. You look for Gavin, but can't see him anywhere! He must be buried under Slag's body!

As tears stain your face, he crawls out. Joyfully, he pulls you free from the dragon's claws and holds you tight. The cavern is suddenly very quiet after all the hissing and roaring.

There is a great clamor at the far end of the cavern. Gavin pulls you behind a pile of crowns and rings and other beautiful things as you watch.

Spears at their back, the caravaners are pushed forward, their hands tied by the band of orcs shoving them in.

"Slag, here is dinner!" the orc leader cries, before he joins his cowardly orcmates in the tunnel. The dazed caravaners stumble around the cavern before they spot Slag and cry in dismay.

You and Gavin appear and comfort them, and then they see that the dragon is dead. Ranth hugs you both, grateful tears in his eyes. Gavin says, "Take that tunnel out, and we'll follow."

Before the orcs can learn that Slag is dead, you run for your freedom through the twisting tunnels. As you reach the surface and fresh air, Gavin grabs and twirls you, his face alight with love.

"Come back with me!" he demands.

"That's not a question," you protest.

"No," he answers, "and neither is this!" And he kisses you soundly while the caravaners murmur happily.

It appears your adventuring days are over—for the moment.

END ADVENTURE

PATHWAY 48

Swallowing your pride, you pretend to stumble and call out sharply, "Ow! Gavin!"

The figure of the tall blond Ranger swerves, and instantly he is running back toward you. Just as he bends down to you, you jump up and race for the tree. Gavin cries out and is on your heels, but too late! You slap your hands first against the bark of the old withered tree and then stand, taking great gulps of air.

"You beat me, but not fairly," Gavin argues as he trots up.

You look up, shaking your long red hair from your neck. "Not fairly? The whole trial was unfair. How could any human hope to outrun an elf? I used my wits instead of my feet, that's all!"

Stormseeker watches, tossing his head up and down. You would swear that he is amused.

Gavin stands in the hot sun, a most unelven gleam in his eyes. "You knew I'd come back for you!"

"That thought occurred to me."

"And what made you think it?"

"I don't know . . . something in your eyes when you talked to me." Suddenly, you are a little nervous. Gavin is acting most peculiar!

"Something in my eyes! Might it be this?" he shouts and grabs you, pulling you to his chest roughly and giving you a sound kiss.

You are aghast as he lets go. Before you can say another word, he grabs you by the waist and tosses you aboard Stormseeker.

"You're going home with me!"

"But—but you promised—"

"Another elven first. I lied." Gavin stands by your boot, his hand on Stormseeker's neck. "You are a thoroughly spoiled, selfish, and annoying human—and one of the most beautiful girls I have ever met. You twist my heart, I, who am not supposed to have a heart! I can't take you on your quest, Tyrna. I'm too afraid of the dangers you might meet. No, I'm going to take you home and see you there safe, then I'll come back to finish the orcs."

"But—"

He places a slender finger across your lips. "Not another word, or I will be forced to silence you again."

Cheeks blushing, you remain quiet as Gavin leads Stormseeker across the wastes. You have conquered the emotions of an elf, but to no avail as he begins the journey to take you home. Yet something in your heart makes you very, very happy.

END ADVENTURE

PATHWAY
49

You race for the doors as Gavin shouts at you again. As one of the brigands charges you, you trip him and leap past. You sprint through the remaining guards and through the columns, Kolroth's men yelling at your heels.

But as you run into the night, you hear the terrible "uhhhh" of the stone troll. It is somewhere in front of you! You hesitate and are grabbed from behind by Kolroth's followers. As you kick and scream, they sling you over the shoulders of the biggest one and carry you back into the temple.

Dismay crosses Gavin's face as you are dumped at Kolroth's feet. The cleric gives an evil smile and opens his mouth. Instead of words, you hear the stone troll's groan. You look at the floor as you realize you've been tricked.

Kolroth laughs. "You wish to be free? Very well,

then. I'll give you a chance to earn it. I'll give you up as sacrifices—if you will do a task for me."

You and Gavin stare at each other. You both know that anything Kolroth wants is likely to be evil, but it might give you another chance to escape rather than being killed on the spot. Your fighter code tells you not to collaborate with wicked beings like Kolroth, though.

Gavin says, "That all depends on what you want us to do."

"No, Gavin," you protest. "He's rotten through and through."

As Kolroth waits, you must decide whether you will agree to the task or not.

1. If you agree to do the evil cleric's task, go to Pathway 27 (page 107).

2. If you refuse, see Pathway 30 (page 119).

PATHWAY
50

You clamp your knees tightly to his flanks. "Run, Stormseeker!" you cry, bending low over his neck.

The magnificent creature begins to race along the ground ahead of the stampede. The bellowing and thunder of the herd are right at your heels, but you manage to stay in front and hang on. As you near the lake, Stormseeker swerves out of their path. You watch as the cattle plow into the waters. One or two flounder helplessly in deep water, unable to get back to shore. It is a sad sight.

At the lake's end, the dam, an immense structure of earth and wood, greets you. It is grotesque, with carved beast heads and lashed with thick rope—clearly of orcish make. They must have a reason for attempting to dam the river, though you can't imagine what.

Stormseeker is too visible. You will be better off

on foot and hiding among the rocks. You slide off. "Thank you, Stormseeker. Go wherever you wish or your master sends you."

The elven horse nuzzles your hand before turning and trotting away.

Common sense tells you to wait for Gavin, and the area looks clear. You could hide and hope to spot caravaners. You are tired and hungry and thirsty and know they must be much worse off in the hands of the orcs.

Your weariness fades suddenly as orcs noisily thrash their way through the brush toward you. From the clubs and bows in their hands, they are looking for dinner. If they find you hiding, it might go ill for you. On the other hand, if you surrender, they might just put you with the caravaners, and half your quest would be over. Your thoughts are interrupted as one of them stumbles over you. You wrestle in the dark as other orcs answer his cries for help. Scared stiff, you kick him in the stomach and he falls aside. You can either let them take you captive or you can run for it and try to wait for Gavin.

1. *If trying to make a run for it and waiting for Gavin seems best, go to Pathway 44 (page 163).*

2. *If you decide to let them take you captive, turn to Pathway 19 (page 75).*

PATHWAY
51

You smile at Loric, as you touch the coronet upon your head. "I'll help you, Loric, but you must . . ." You stop, trying to remember what it is you wanted to say. "You must be good . . ." You stop again. The treasure glows in front of you. It is power! The two of you will be able to sweep across the desert in front of a mighty army—no, that isn't what you were thinking!

You look at the handsome fighter, as the red-gold curse of the dragon gold sweeps through your thoughts. You will be his dragon queen, but only because you cannot bear to leave the treasure. Although you try, you cannot remember why it is you came to be there, only that you will never leave.

You are doomed to spend the rest of your life in those underground caves while Loric's dream of creating a new empire wastes away.

END ADVENTURE

PATHWAY 52

You press your heels to Stormseeker. "Then follow me!" you say, with a good deal more courage than you feel. The stallion tosses his head in protest, but carries you across the sands nearer the great wooden dam.

It is immense. You gulp at its size. Behind it, the waters spill into the desert wasteland, leaving a great dark stain on the sands. Despite your urging, the horse stops in his tracks. Gavin, a little out of breath, places his hand on the stallion's dapple-gray neck.

His face is twisted. "Wasted," he says bitterly. "All that water—wasted."

"But won't it help wherever it touches?"

"Yes . . . and no. Whatever grows there now will be too flooded to thrive, and there are some areas of the wastes so blasted by the blue dragon Slag that their evil keeps any good from happening. The valleys of my people need that water!"

Cut into the ground is the mouth of a huge tunnel. The watergate towers above it, its cruel spikes pointing at the sky. It is bound with ropes as thick as your arm, and though it looks as though it could be cut open, letting the water down into the original riverbed, it would also flood the tunnel and the captives, if they are being held below. Without saying a word to each other, it is clear the tunnel will have to be entered.

Gavin prepares to go. You shudder. The thought of being underground and in the dark suddenly frightens you. Stormseeker stamps impatiently in the brush.

"Make me a torch," you ask the Ranger, breaking off a limb of the shrub as you slide to the ground.

He frowns. "Do you wish to blind me?"

"Better you than me," you sputter, embarrassed.

"Why not stand in the tunnel mouth and shout to all the orcs that you're coming in? Tyrna, you're being really stupid."

Your face is turning red. "I am not! Do you expect me to stumble around when I can't even see? How do you expect me to draw my sword and fight if something happens? You can go ahead or follow behind, but I'm not going anywhere that I can't see!"

Gavin grabs you by the shoulders and shakes you as he would a child. Your head jerks back and forth until you think your brains rattle—and your head has already hurt all day. You burst into tears and fiercely try to brush them away. You're too old to cry, though you're not exactly sure why you want to.

He stops. "I'm sorry!" He adds humbly, "There isn't anything to be afraid of, Tyrna, if you would only trust me a little."

Trust somebody who just tried to shake your head from your shoulders? You stare at him, hoping your face isn't all red and blotchy. Your chin sticks out a little the way it used to when your father scolded you.

Gavin sighs. "If you can't trust me to guide you down, then go back and follow me around the lake to the waterfall. I can let you use a torch in there most of the way. Tyrna, be sensible. Or give up this crazy idea of yours and come home with me." He takes your chin between his fingers so that you must look into his deep violet eyes. "Let me take care of you, always. I promise that I'll bring back fighters to rescue the caravaners. Remember, I came this far to be with you."

You don't want to be trapped in a passage that you can't see in. You move your head and he lets go of you, but the warmth of his fingers remains. "I can't do it!" You stop, as he groans in exasperation. You ask, "What makes you so sure the waterfall tunnel might come close to the dam?"

The wind shifts. His elven-gold hair blows gently. "The lair of the blue dragon Slag runs underneath the foot of the mountains. All his tunnels and all his treasure lie below us."

"Gold! Dragon gold and jewels! No wonder the orcs are mining here," you say thoughtfully. "And you knew it all the time," you add accusingly.

He does not answer.

Anger drives away your fear for a moment. The treasure of the dead monster lured the evil orcs across the desert to kill your father! You curl your hand around your sword hilt. "We'll face an army, sooner or later."

"Perhaps, but I prefer later."

"Because I am a girl and you don't think I can hold my own?"

"No!" A tortured word breaks from him. He takes you by the shoulders. "Because you have awakened the human side of my feelings. I am only half elf, Tyrna. My mother was a human girl who chose to follow my father back to the valleys. I could not bear to see you hurt." He cups the side of your face gently, then releases you. He clears his throat. "Please," he says again. "Trust me."

You must decide if you will put your life and quest in his hands, or if you will admit that you might be wrong and backtrack to the waterfall, Gavin's preferred route.

As you stare into his face, you realize there is a desire in you to go home, anybody's home, to be safe for a while. The grand adventure you started out on, to go to the Warrior Games, has turned very sour. The world is a harder place than you imagined. You wonder if you are cut out to be a fighter after all. Gavin has pledged to you that he will save the caravaners. You could let him carry out your quest for you. But the thought nags at you. You are Sword Daughter and can't let anyone else do the job that falls to you. As he waits, you know you must give him your answer: trust him and go on, return to the waterfall, or go home with him.

1. *If you go home, see Pathway 16 (page 66).*
2. *If you change your mind about the waterfall passage and tell him so, turn to Pathway 7 (page 33).*
3. *But if you decide to get as close to the damworks as possible and trust Gavin to lead you through the dark, turn to Pathway 4 (page 20).*

PATHWAY 53

"Will you kill an orc for me?"

Slag lowers his snout close to you, amber eyes glowing. "I will do whatever you wish!"

"All right then." You step forward, drawing your sword to break the shackles open. You're sure that you are still in control. As you look over the chains and shackles, you see that they are dented and marred by teeth marks. Slag has chewed in vain for many years!

"Look at me," Slag commands softly.

You look up, into his luminous eyes. They are as soft yellow as gold, molten and free in the dark . . . and you are lost. Slag has you completely in his power!

The dragon opens his jaws in a reptile grin. "You're mine now! I think I'll make a dragon queen of you. It will be sweet to fly the skies again. You'll ride my back and we'll conquer the world together! Now open my chains."

From faraway, you hear a voice calling, "No, Tyrna! Don't! This is Gavin. Hold on, I'm coming to help you!"

Who is Gavin? You wonder faintly as you place your sword in the lock and break it open. For that matter, who is Tyrna? The blue dragon rears in triumph.

END ADVENTURE

PATHWAY 54

"Gavin!" you yell, as you race deep into the mysterious tunnel.

The cleric throws his arms up. "No, fools! Don't go that way!"

Gavin joins you. He trips and falls and scrambles up quickly, his hands grasping something.

"What is it?"

"Dragon scale! We may be in trouble ahead!" He drops the object and helps you to run through the darkened tunnel. It is immense. The pounding footsteps of the cleric at your heels echo and thunder about you as you run for your lives.

The tunnel opens suddenly into a huge chamber, a dragon's den! You flee inward, tumbling through heaps of gold and treasure.

Kolroth stops just outside, jumping up and down in anger. Gavin helps you to your feet and you look up. There is a shaft of light gleaming from above, from a crack in the chamber roof so high that it must be part of the mountaintop. It stabs downward, setting the dragon gold afire with radiance.

The cleric does not enter—it's as though an invisible wall prevents him. Gavin approaches the entrance. With the tip of your sword, he points out lettering etched into the stone arch.

"Only the pure of heart may enter," he reads.

"Well, that solves that mystery. He must be anything but," you say, looking at the cleric. You glance around. "Neron must have enchanted this place, to keep out treasure hunters."

"Possibly. This was Slag's lair. Why, the treasure here is higher than you, even if you stood on my shoulders!"

The two of you stop talking as the cleric's voice reaches you.

"Now, my pretties! I can't get in—but neither can you get out!" He smiles evilly and strokes his beard. "Bring me that bottle and a bit of treasure, and I'll let you pass freely."

"Don't trust him," Gavin mutters.

"I don't intend to—not for a minute," you agree.

Kolroth says, in a honeyed voice, "Don't give up a fortune so quickly! Power, wealth, anything your heart desires! I'll let you take as much as you can carry—only bring me that bottle!"

You grasp it firmly. "Never! Besides"—and you blush as you look at Gavin—"I already have what my heart desires."

His face lights with joy as he reaches out and takes

your hand. "And I! We'll get out of here, Kolroth, one way or another, never fear!" He points upward. "Even if we have to climb out!"

You set the bottle down on the treasure pile. "This looks like an excellent place to keep it from evil hands!"

As you release the bottle, the mountain rumbles. Gavin holds you close, while a huge rock rolls away from the chamber side. Sunlight floods in, along with fresh air, and you hear Stormseeker's ringing neigh.

As the rays of sun hit the cursed dragon gold, it begins to hiss and sizzle. Gavin pulls you outside. The cleric's curses scream after you.

As you reach safety, and the dapple-gray stallion's side, you turn and look. With a puff of dust and a great explosion, the mountain collapses. Slag's End, the cursed treasure, and the evil cleric are buried for all time.

END ADVENTURE

PATHWAY
55

"**N**o!" you shout, throwing the coronet from you. "My father is the man your orcs killed!" You dash forward and seize a mighty sword from the treasure pile.

Loric stares in surprise. His hands fumble for his sword hilt.

You think you see a shadowy figure darting behind him, among the troop of Loric's cutthroats and orcs. Could it be Gavin?

You point your sword at Loric's throat. "You have killed. You have dammed the river Ashkaraneth! You should be punished for your crimes."

Loric laughs in amusement. "And who will do that?" The laughter of his men joins his. He bats your sword away and draws his own.

You back up cautiously, knowing that the weapon you have is far too heavy for your slender wrists to

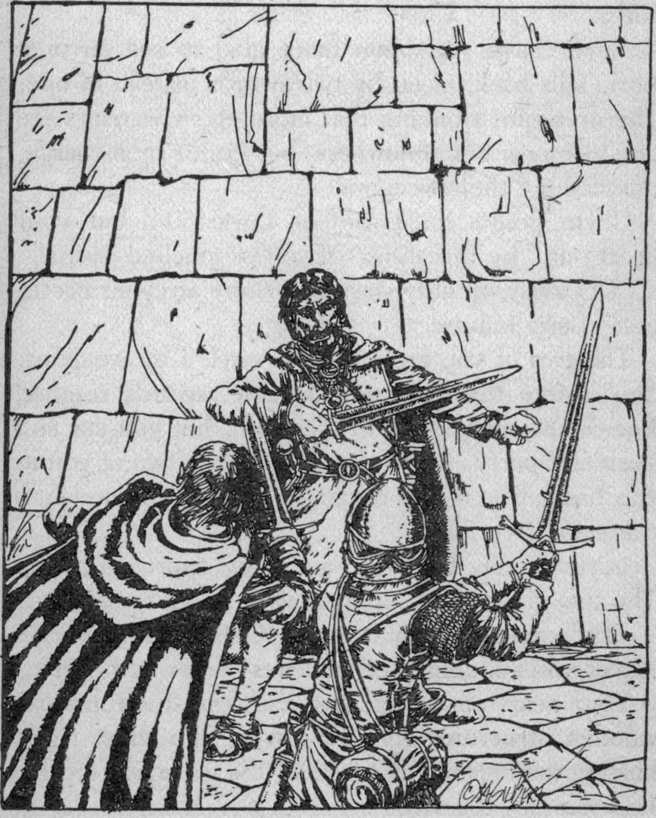

wield for very long. Loric crosses his sword with yours, and the metal clangs.

An elven war cry splits the air! Gavin bounds from out of nowhere. "Come, come, my brothers!" he adds.

Never have you been more glad to see anyone! Loric falls back, faced by two swords instead of one. The orcs run, thinking that more elven warriors are due to appear out of nowhere, but Loric's men charge, brandishing their weapons.

Gavin points his sword at Loric. "I'll cut your heart out." he threatens, "if you've touched Tyrna!"

"Cut away, mighty warrior! Where are your brothers?" Loric taunts.

The two of you are suddenly circled by weapons. You charge through, side by side, swords ringing! Each blow shakes you to the teeth, but you cut and slash and parry. Brigands run from the two of you as you break free of the dragon treasure room and into the main cavern.

Loric signals his men, and they approach again. The two of you back up until you can go no farther.

"The dam," Gavin orders. "Cut the ropes!" He leaves you suddenly and matches blades with Loric.

Your heart pounding, you scurry up the immense wooden structure. As you saw at the thick ropes holding the logs tightly together, the watergate groans. Its voice fills the air.

Loric and Gavin are face to face, their blades locked in deathly struggle. But Loric looks up at you. He springs back, crying, "Run for it! The dam's open!"

He and his men charge away.

Gavin appears below you. "Jump, Tyrna!" He catches you and kisses you soundly before letting you go. "Hurry! I found the caravaners! We may have enough time to free them!"

You race through the tunnel as the watergate continues to moan. Cracks like explosions pop your ears. Gavin bends over the forms of exhausted caravaners, his sword cutting their bonds. You hurry, your hands shaking in your excitement to loosen them.

Gavin catches you up again, as the caves become silent. The watergate has held, but you are all free. The caravaners run in the direction Gavin points out to them, but Gavin holds you back. In most un-elven joy, he holds you tightly.

"Come back with me—I can't lose you now!" As he kisses you firmly, you melt into his arms. He is strong and handsome and kind and gentle, all the treasures you could ever have wished for yourself!

"I'll come," you tell him.

As he takes your hand and the two of you run through the tunnels to freedom, you know that your father has been avenged with honor, and that Gavin will never rest until the Ashkaraneth is flowing once more. As for yourself—to serve with and for love has always been an honorable destiny.

END ADVENTURE

PATHWAY
56

Before Gavin can say a word, you pull your sword. "I came to fight," you declare brashly, and jump out in front of the approaching beasts.

The orcs snarl and cry, seizing their own weapons. Gavin joins you, a grim expression on his face. "You and your temper," he mutters, even as swords ring as he parries a blow.

The orcs scatter, yelling in surprise. You run after them as they dart inside the blue tunnel and beyond into a tremendous cavern.

Much to your surprise, you run right under the snout of an immense blue dragon! The orcs run in circles, yelling oaths and brandishing their swords and clubs as the dragon snorts in astonishment. The air crackles as he looses his lightning-bolt breath! Slag is not dead but lives imprisoned below the waters of the Ashkaraneth!

Gavin pulls you back, as the blue dragon rattles his chains and strains at the crystal pillars that hold the roof. The roof is the crystal basin of the lake itself! The dragon thrashes madly, his body hacked with cuts as the orcs try to defend themselves.

You rush forward as the dragon blasts an orc and begins to swallow him, exposing his own throat as he eats. Gavin at your side, you aim at Slag's only vulnerable spot in a body of blue armor.

The dragon coughs and chokes, his tail thrashing around. It slams into you, knocking you across the cavern. As you stagger back to your feet, Gavin dodges a crackling blue bolt and throws his sword. It arches through the air and sinks deep into its target! With a shuddering hiss, the dragon crashes to the floor. His immense form tears a crystal column loose.

The orcs stop running around and immediately begin to stuff treasure inside their purses and coats. They cuff and argue over the dragon gold, as the roof groans and sags.

Gavin grabs you. "Come on! The roof will cave in!"

He tears your bow from your back and shoots a climbing line deep into the side of the cavern wall. You climb, and none too quickly, as thunder booms through the chamber! The roof gives way and tons of water pour in. Gavin shinnies up the rope and the two of you cling to the top, bowed against what remains of the crystal basin roof as the lake floods the cavern.

The water crashes up around you, and Gavin cuts you loose. "You'll float to the top!" he cries, as the waters grab and swirl you away.

You gasp and choke for air and are suddenly bobbing on the lake surface. It is a long moment, then Gavin's blond head breaks through also. There is not a sign of the orcs, weighed down by their greed and dragon treasure.

As you swim to the shore, there is, alas, also no sign of the caravaners. But the force of the cavern's flooding has burst the dam open and the river once again flows in its bed. Gavin swims to you and pulls you close. "Don't you ever do anything like that again!" he says angrily.

"And why not?" you sputter indignantly, spitting out lake water. Your hair is loose and floats around you like an auburn cloud.

Gavin playfully gathers a fistful of it and draws your face to his. "Because I love you, that's why! And I'm tired of watching you risk your neck when I ought to be protecting you!" And he seals your lips with a kiss before you can protest.

END ADVENTURE

PATHWAY
57

As Kolroth grasps for the bottle, you do a back flip away from him. The cleric jumps back, startled by your stunt. Then he leaps at you, and the two of you roll among the treasure. Sharp jewels dig into your back and sides as the cleric tries to rake your face with his clawlike nails. Gavin calls out in alarm as you twist free.

Once on your feet, you race into the passageway, dodging the dank tunnel. Kolroth laughs evilly as he chases after you. Torchlight flickers in front of you, and deep water ripples ahead. You stop short of the pond. Its evil-looking waters boil as mandibles click!

"Look out, Tyrna!" Gavin shouts frantically. He cuts between you and the cleric as you totter on the underground pond's edge. His slender body trips the cleric, who falls with a scream into the oily waters.

Ferocious water beetles charge at him and drag

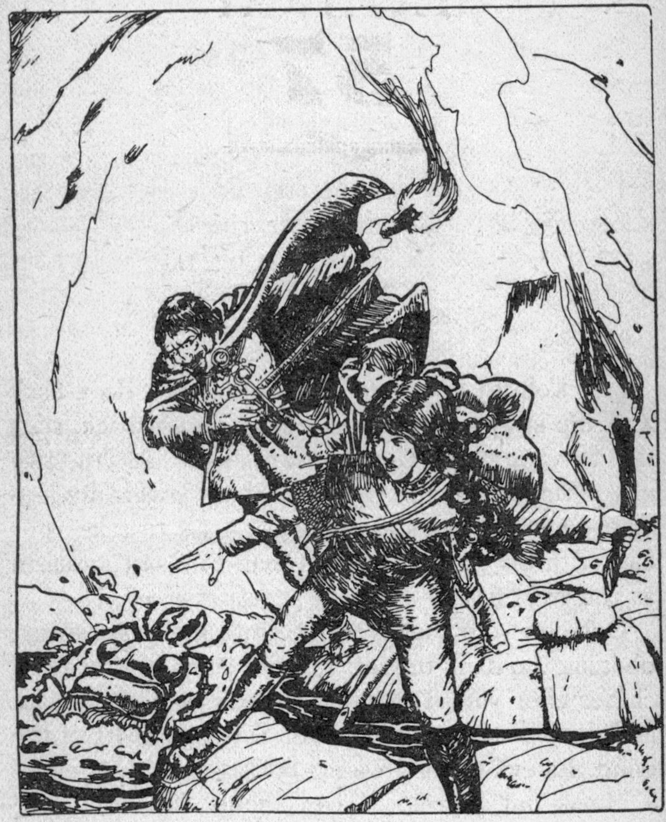

him under, bubbles and froth following their disappearance. It is the last of Kolroth.

Gavin grabs you. "I thought you were done for!" He holds you back and looks you up and down. "Are you all right?"

"Yes," you answer, shaken. "I think so." You look at the potion in your hand. "He would have done anything for this." You shudder.

You drop the potion into the apparently bottomless pond. The waters dance and suddenly grow sparkling clear again. Gavin shouts for joy.

"The Ashkaraneth is free again!" He hugs you tightly.

"Yes." You look into the wellhead, sadness creeping through you. "My quest is finished . . . but I'll always remember you."

Gavin laughs. How can he laugh at your parting? His arms pull you ever closer, as he bends his face down to yours. "You're not going anywhere without me!" he tells you and seals his promise with his lips upon yours.

END ADVENTURE

PATHWAY 58

You nudge Gavin. "Don't forget—you're an elf! They'll spot you right away."

"You're right."

The two of you make your way to the chamber. It is a huge hall, carved out of the stone. A long table runs down the center, surrounded by high-backed chairs fit for kings.

"What is this place?" you whisper, awed.

Gavin shakes his head in bewilderment.

Tallow candles barely light the hall. The two of you walk cautiously through the shadows, feeling afraid in spite of yourselves. There is a door, cracked open, at the other end. The doorway is massive, carved from wood, big enough for a giant to step through.

Suddenly, the mumbling starts again. You and Gavin stop. Your pulse is racing.

A man lumbers up from the middle chair. His clothes and furs are old, though he is young. He weaves drunkenly toward you, a crooked gold crown on his head.

"Ghosts! Ghosts be you! Get away from here and leave me alone!"

Gavin pulls you back toward him, as the man staggers closer. His eyes are crazed, and a chill runs down your back.

"Give me back my kingdom or let me be! The treasure does me no good now! Answer me, I tell you! I order you in the name of Loric . . . me!" He belches and throws aside his jug. He draws his broadsword and brandishes it in front of him as he comes closer.

Gavin whispers, "Run for it!" He picks up Loric's discarded cloak, lying on the floor. "Back to the orcs, if you can." However, he draws his own sword.

You look in both directions. You're nearest the end now, with the door standing ajar. Its only advantage is that you know it doesn't lead back to the orcs . . . but where it does go is a mystery. There is an eerie blue glow beyond it.

"Run!" Gavin yells, as the madman charges. He sidesteps Loric easily. The madman rolls to the floor and scrambles to pick up his dropped weapon. Which way will you go?

1. *If you decide to chance the door, turn to Pathway 29 (page 115).*

2. *See Pathway 39 (page 146) if you go back the way you came in and join the carousing orcs.*

About the Author

RHONDI VILOTT first got hooked on writing in third grade and spent most of her school years working on the school newspaper and in creative writing. She first began working on fantasy and science fiction in the 1970s, and attended the Clarion SF Writer's Workshop in 1979.

Although she has written romances for teens and adults, science fiction is her first love. And although most writers claim poetic license, Rhondi likes to think she has a pilot's license—for flights of fantasy.

Rhondi lives with her husband, Howard, and their four children in California, and warns all her children's friends that anything they say may be used in a book about them.

JOIN THE *DRAGONTALES* READER'S PANEL

Help us bring you more of the books you like by filling out this survey and mailing it in today.

1. Book title: _____

   Book #: _____

2. Using the scale below, how would you rate this book on the following features? Please write in one rating from 0-10 for each feature in the spaces provided.

POOR		NOT SO GOOD			O.K.			GOOD		EXCELLENT
0	1	2	3	4	5	6	7	8	9	10

RATING

Overall opinion of book...................... ____
Plot/Story .... ____
Writing style .... ____
Suspense .... ____
Main characters
        Hero .... ____
        Heroine .... ____
Scene on front cover......................... ____
Colors of front cover........................ ____

3. Which endings did you like best? _____
_____

4. How likely are you to buy another title in the *Dragontales* series? (Circle one number on the scale below.)

DEFINITELY NOT BUY	PROBABLY NOT BUY	NOT SURE	PROBABLY BUY	DEFINITELY BUY
0 1	2 3	4 5 6	7 8	9 10

5. Listed below are various fantasy lines. Rate only those you have read using the 0-10 scale below.

POOR	NOT SO GOOD		O.K.		GOOD		EXCELLENT
0 1	2 3	4	5	6	7 8	9	10

RATING

CHOOSE YOUR OWN ADVENTURE .... _____
DRAGONTALES .... _____
ENDLESS QUEST .... _____
FIGHTING FANTASY .... _____
_____ .... _____
_____ .... _____

5. Where do you usually buy your books (check one or more):
- ( ) Bookstore
- ( ) Supermarket
- ( ) Variety Store
- ( ) Drug Store
- ( ) Discount Store
- ( ) Department Store
- ( ) Other:_____

6. About how many fantasy paperback books have you bought for yourself in the past six months?

Approximate #: _____

7. What is your age? _____   Sex: ( ) Male
( ) Female

8. What are your two favorite magazines?

1) _____

2) _____

If you would like to participate in future research projects, please complete the following:

PRINT NAME:_____

ADDRESS:_____

CITY:_____STATE_____ZIP_____

PHONE: ( ) _____

Thank you. Please send to New American Library, Fantasy Research Department, 1633 Broadway, New York, New York 10019.